KEY OF
THE DARKHOUSE

DEBORAH ZELASNY

DEDICATION

For my son, Jake,
who encouraged me to publish this book.
You will always be the key to my heart.

PROLOGUE

W ere it not for the birds that dotted the craggy rocks and splashed into the frigid sea water, Graystone Island would have simply been invisible. There was not a patch of green earth anywhere on its shoreline, camouflaging it with the Baric Sea. It melted into the colorless waters of the ocean as if it had been painted there by a melancholy artist hundreds of years ago. And although it appeared haunted and desolate, Graystone Island was very much inhabited.

The citizens of Graystone Island were just as drab and lifeless as the rocks they lived upon. They were cold, expressionless people, hardened by the frigid Baric winds that swept into their homes at night.

But those *birds*- the bright-billed puffins that cavorted on the pebbly shore, the shimmery white bodies of the terns- they upset the gray balance of the island and provided color and noise to a monochromatic landscape. And perhaps it was the presence of these birds that kept young Key Terek alive through the years.

Ever since he was a child, Key would wander around the rocks, sketching the puffins and seagulls in a small notebook. They kept him colorful inside and allowed him to dream of a life far away from the Baric Sea.

Key lived with his father, Lorn, in a black tower at the north end of Graystone Island. The tower was designed to be a lighthouse, a beacon to guide ships through the darkest nights. But Key's father refused to illuminate the lighthouse. Lorn Terek believed that no ship should venture too close to Graystone Island and no foreigners should set foot upon their shores. The other islanders supported his beliefs, so the lighthouse remained dark for decades. It became known, fittingly enough, as the Darkhouse.

Key lived and breathed in the Darkhouse for all of his young life, knowing that ships sank and sailors drowned because there was no light to guide them past the jagged rocks of Graystone Island. He dreamed of lighting the Darkhouse and saving weary travelers, but he never dared to do it. He would never go against his father. The punishment would be just too much to bear.

At sixteen years of age, Key was strong and handsome. He had black hair and deep, dark eyes that reflected every shade of the churning gray sea. He hardly ever smiled, and his eyebrows were always creased together in constant thought. Inside, his heart ached with a constant longing that he could never extinguish. There was so much he yearned for, yet it all seemed out of reach.

"I want to travel away from this place," he told his father. "I want to see The Green Islands."

But Lorn only laughed.

"There is nothing to see!" his father snapped. "Just rocks and ocean. It's impossible to reach The Green Islands- they are thousands of miles away. You were born to stay here and fish."

Key despised fishing but it was his sole responsibility in life. He inherited the job from his father as soon as he turned twelve. Fishing in the Baric was a horribly difficult task, for there were many mouths to feed and not many fish. There were no boats on the island, so Key had to find ways to fish without leaving land. He learned to throw nets and set traps, and knew which bait would lure the biggest fish. He discovered secrets by watching birds dive for meals, and followed them to their prime fishing locations every morning. That was how he saw the disaster. Or rather, *heard* it.

CHAPTER 1

It was almost dawn, and Key was crouched on the tip of a black shale, watching terns circle the sea. A thick, gray fog blanketed the sky, so it was difficult to spot the birds when they flew too high. He could feel the fog all around him, creeping into his lungs and blurring his eyes. It was common for a morning fog to appear across the Baric, so Key was used to relying on his ears instead of his eyes. He knew the calls of seagulls, as well as terns and plovers. The puffins were often strangely quiet, but he knew where to find them. It was easy for him to recognize a foreign sound, like the crash that rang through the air that foggy morning.

It sounded like a building crumbling, with wood splintering and splashing into the water below. Groans and creaks echoed in the silence, intertwined with lapping ocean waves. Key knew what he heard was a shipwreck; a boat being torn apart by the jagged coastline of Graystone Island. He stood and squinted, but could only see blurry shadows in the fog. From somewhere far out at sea, he heard muffled screams and shouting -a quick shriek- then silence. Key jumped from rock to rock, desperate to help. He listened for what seemed like an eternity.

Key collapsed onto the pebbly shore and lay his head in his hands. The sea was silent now and the fog lifted, but voices from the wreck still echoed in his mind. The water lapped at his feet, and all around him the puffins perched on their rocks, waiting.

"*Help me*," a weak voice called over the waves. Key lifted his head, certain he had imagined the voice until he heard it again. "*Please.*"

He looked around but saw no one, just birds and splintered wood from the wreck. He scanned the island, but it was only gray, dark with shadows.

"Hello?" he said aloud, waiting for a response.

He heard nothing so he leapt onto the shales for a better view. He stopped when he heard the voice again, which was now right at his feet.

"*Help me.*"

He bent over and peered beneath the shallow cliff, and there he saw a figure clinging to a slippery rock near the shore.

"I'm coming!" he called, his heart leaping at the thought of a survivor. "Hang on! Don't let go!"

Key ran to the water's edge. The rocks here were as sharp as spears, so he removed his boots and carefully waded into the icy water.

The stranded figure was not far ahead, but he felt hope fleeting away from him. The person looked like a rag doll, twisted and sprawled against the rocks with pieces of wood and debris gathering around them. The word *'dead'* immediately popped into his mind, but he kept on swimming as fast as he could. He felt his sweater snagging on sharp rocks beneath him, and several times his knees knocked against stones, but he kept going.

He quickly reached the rock and realized that the twisted survivor was a girl. She did not look much older than himself, and had long, light brown hair that lay in wet ringlets across her back. He did not ask her name or if she was alright. He offered no supportive words or comforting reassurances. He simply slipped a strong arm around her neck and began pulling her to shore. She looked and felt like a lifeless stone- her lips were blue and parted, her face streaked with blood. She gave no resistance and did not paddle to safety beside him. Her limbs were motionless, drifting beneath the water as he pulled her along. *Dead*, his mind told him again, *dead*. But he clenched his teeth and struggled to reach the shore, determined to do something right. *If only I can save this one girl,* the thought, *if only I can bring her back to life.*

Key reached land and dragged the girl's lifeless body across the smooth pebbles. He heard a short, raspy gurgle emerge from her throat, so he quickly turned her sideways to let the water spill from her mouth. She sputtered and coughed, and he could feel her warm breath on his hand. Key sighed with relief and quickly retrieved his boots, cringing as his wet feet pressed into the dry leather. Then he gathered her up in his arms, intent on taking her to the town doctor. He did not mind that he had to carry her all the way there. He took no notice of the chill settling in his bones or the wet clothes that clung to his body like icy claws. He was just relieved and astonished that she was still alive, and held her close to his chest in gratitude. The puffins watched him carry the limp body of the sea girl towards town, with the wet hem of her brightly colored dress dragging along the ground behind him.

CHAPTER 2

The Kind Doctor, as he was known to most of the islanders, lived in a small stone cottage not far from the Darkhouse. His name was Samuel Alcid, and he had been the doctor of Graystone Island for half a century. Key believed him to be the only good-hearted man on the island, and often went to him for advice or conversation. But today was different. As he frantically rang the bell that hung from a rope outside the doctor's door, Key prayed that the Kind Doctor could offer more than advice this time. *This time* he needed a savior.

The door to the doctor's cottage whipped open, and there stood Samuel's wife, Nanny, drying her hands with a dish towel. Her mouth stretched into a smile at the sight of Key on her doorstep, but quickly faded when she set eyes on his condition and the drenched girl in his arms.

"Lord, child, what happened?" she cried, pulling Key inside, immediately leading him to the doctor's office.

Key followed Nanny into the warm cottage, savoring the smell of her home, which was so unlike the dampness of the Darkhouse.

"Key!" Samuel exclaimed upon seeing the boy in his office. The doctor looked like he had just rolled out of bed, with gray hair sticking straight out above his ears, and a shade of early morning stubble on his chin. "Who is this? What happened?"

Key placed the girl gently across the doctor's examining table. He was out of breath and quite shaken, but he did his best to explain everything that had happened out in the Baric Sea.

"It's impossible to navigate our waters in the darkness," Samuel sighed as he examined the girl. "She needed light."

"I know," Key said, shivering, dripping water onto the doctor's stone floor.

The doctor glanced at his guest, hearing shame in the boy's voice. Samuel smiled sympathetically, placing a hand on Key's shoulder. "Let Nanny clean you up and make you some tea," Samuel suggested. "I will tend to the girl."

Key nodded, his eyes focused on the survivor. "Please help her," he said sadly, his energy drained. "She has to live."

The doctor nodded. "I'll take care of her."

Nanny wrapped a blanket around Key's shoulders and led him out of the office.

"I couldn't let her drown," Key muttered.

"I know, Key, I know," she said, patting his shoulder. "Let's get you dry."

***

Key was sitting by the fire, naked beneath layers of soft, quilted blankets. His hair was still damp with sea water, but his clothes were quickly drying near the hearth. He had not said a word since pleading for Samuel's help, and sat motionless, staring into the fire, wondering about the girl's condition.

"Key?" Samuel said.

"Samuel!" Key exclaimed, startled by the doctor's entrance. He wanted to jump to his feet but feared the blanket would slip out of his hands. "Is she all right?"

Samuel smiled, wiping his glasses with the edge of his sweater. "She's a strong one. But she-"

"She's all right now?" Key asked hopefully. "She'll live?"

"Yes, " Samuel nodded, "She will live. But, Key-"

Key laughed with relief, holding out a strong hand for the doctor to shake. "Thank you, Samuel! Thank you so much!"

"I want you to know something, though, Key," the doctor tried to explain again. "Your survivor has been through an ordeal, a trauma. She's asleep now but she was quite shaken. She's not from these parts, that's obvious. I don't know how she'll fare when she wakes up."

Key didn't seem fazed. "Well, I'll be back," he assured the doctor. "I'll check on her every day. I'll make sure she's okay. She *has* to be okay."

He wanted to go in and see her, but the doctor insisted she needed rest. So Key gathered up his clothes and headed back out into the world, knowing he must finish fishing before it grew too late.

The morning seemed so different now. The air was cool and the foggy mist had vanished. Broken remains of the shipwreck littered the pebbly shore and Key retrieved pieces as he walked. He nodded to the puffins and waved to the shearwaters that circled above. He wondered if they sensed change in the air, something different, something new. What would she say when she awoke?

CHAPTER 3

*S**LAP!** A strong, hard hand struck Key's face with a powerful sting. He clenched his teeth but said nothing.

"How dare you!" his father shouted, an echo spinning up the high, black walls of the Darkhouse. "How *dare* you rescue that girl? Do you know the villagers *saw* you with her? *Saw* you carrying her across the island? *What an embarrassment you are!* Is this how you respect your father? What kind of son are you?"

"Father," Key pleaded. "She was drowning. She needed my help. I couldn't just leave her there."

"She's a *foreigner!*" Lorn shouted. "You know we cannot have foreigners on this island. *They will pollute our whole population!*"

Key sighed and shook his head, knowing he could never make his father understand. "If the Darkhouse had been lit," Key began, "the ship wouldn't have crashed on the rocks! She could have seen through the fog-"

"Are you saying this is *my* fault?" his father snapped. "It's *my* fault that she couldn't steer past the rocks? If she didn't know the ways of the sea then she shouldn't have been sailing!"

"But the fog was thick, and you know our reefs are like spears!" Key argued.

Key's father silenced him with another blow to the face. Key stumbled backwards but he did not cry.

"The Elders will be ashamed of you!" his father hissed. "You wait till they come, you wait and see what they say to you!"

Key turned his back on Lorn, ignoring his threats. Graystone Island was rich with superstition. It was a curse for life if an Elder expressed shame towards a relative, but Key was not afraid.

"The Elders will not be ashamed," Key assured his father. "There is nothing to be ashamed of."

"Disobeying your father?" Lorn asked. "Disrespecting the beliefs of the islanders- *that* is not shameful? The Elders will be disgusted by your behavior. They will curse you!"

"I am not trying to put you to shame, father," Key attempted to explain. "I just wanted to save the girl. I could not let her die."

"And why not?" Lorn questioned. "Because there's too much of your mother in you, that's why!"

"Leave mother out of this," Key growled.

"Believe me, boy, I would be very happy to leave your mother out of this," Lorn said bitterly, "but the very sight of you reminds me of her."

Key shook his head. A large, swollen bruise was forming near his right eye, and his cheek throbbed with pain.

"Mother would have been proud of me," Key said with a deep sigh. Then he turned and walked out of the Darkhouse, leaving Lorn alone with his anger.

Key headed towards shore, but the voice of his father echoed after him:

"You put me to shame!"

Key kept right on walking, thinking only of the girl and the sea, and the lonely gray island that he was forced to call home.

CHAPTER 4

The Kind Doctor was worried. The shipwreck survivor woke shortly before dawn, and since then, she had not said a word. She sat huddled in the corner of the doctor's office, refusing to answer any questions. Nanny even tried to bring the girl some food, which wound up splattered across the office wall.

"Please, child, we're only trying to help," Nanny said soothingly. "I know you're frightened, but we won't hurt you. We're just two kind old folk, the doctor and me."

But the girl remained crouched on the floor, clutching some blankets around her chest. She sat with her head propped against the wall, as if she hadn't the strength to hold it up herself.

"Where am I?" the girl asked in a whispery, far-away voice.

Sam and Nanny tried to explain, but she did not listen. They offered food and clothing, since she was still wearing the tattered remains of a colorful dress, but she refused.

"My parents," the girl said aloud. "Where are my parents?"

"Were they on the boat with you, dear?" Nanny asked.

The girl looked at the doctor's wife in confusion. "The boat?"

"Yes," Sam nodded. "The boat you were sailing on."

The girl paused for a moment, then closed her eyes. Tears dripped down her cheeks, and her bottom lip trembled slightly. "The boat," she repeated again.

"We want to help you, dear," Samuel said sadly. "Do you remember what happened?"

"Where am I?" the girl asked, standing up. "Where are my parents?"

"You're on Graystone Island," Nanny answered. "In the Baric."

The girl turned her head at the mention of the sea. "We made it to the Baric?"

"Your ship crashed on the rocks, child," Samuel explained in a soft voice. "One of our islanders saved you."

"There were no rocks!" she cried. "There was no island! There was only fog and sea. You *lie*!!"

Samuel looked at Nanny nervously. "Graystone is known for being somewhat...*hidden*," Nanny said.

"Hidden?" the girl repeated. "That's ridiculous! This is nonsense. Where is my father? He will tell you himself."

Sam and Nanny did not answer. The girl looked at their faces, searching for an explanation.

"Get my mother, then," she demanded, panic rising in her voice. "Get them both! Bring them here!"

Silence followed, and Samuel stepped forward. "You are the only one who was found."

The girl's eyes widened in shock. "No!" she cried.

Sam and Nanny remained quiet, shaking their heads.

"NO!" she yelled again. "*NO!*"

***

Key arrived at the Kind Doctor's cottage just in time to hear the heart-wrenching scream of the shipwreck survivor. He burst through the door and ran to the back office. The girl sat hunched over on the floor, sobbing uncontrollably. Sam and Nanny were beside her, trying to offer comfort.

"Oh, Key, thank goodness," Nanny exclaimed upon seeing him. She immediately noticed the bruises on his face but said nothing. "Maybe you can help."

She quickly explained what had happened since the survivor had opened her eyes. Samuel approached, abandoning his attempt to soothe the girl. He, too, noticed Key's battered face and cleared his throat uneasily.

"Perhaps we should let you talk to her for a while," Samuel suggested.

"What can *I* do?" Key asked, glancing at the survivor.

"Show her a little compassion, lad," Nanny smiled. "Maybe she'll accept it from you."

Key looked at the doctor's wife skeptically.

"We'll leave you alone with her for a while," Samuel said. "Give us a shout if you have any trouble."

Key opened his mouth to protest, but the Kind Doctor and his wife were already out the door. Nanny turned and gave him a sympathetic smile before closing the door and vanishing into the cottage. Key was alone.

He stared at the girl for a few minutes. She was sitting on the floor with her head against the wall. Her long, brown hair was twisted and knotted from the ordeal, and her lips trembled slightly. Key was certain that he had never seen anyone quite like her. Her skin was darker than his, as if she had spent years in the bright sunlight. She was wrapped in a gray, woolen blanket, but the edge of her colorful dress lay draped across her bare feet.

"Hello," Key said.

The girl did not respond.

He walked slowly towards her, the same way he approached sea birds in the morning. He felt like she would fly away if he moved too quickly.

"My name is Key Terek," he said, crouching down beside her. "I want to tell you what happened."

The girl did not respond. She sat motionless against the wall, her face hidden by her hair.

"You were out at sea," he continued, "and you had an accident. I don't know who you were with or how many people were aboard your ship. I only found you."

The girl flinched at the sound of his words. Her eyes met his, and she instantly sprang to her feet.

"You were lying against a rock in the water," Key explained further. "I looked for others but you were alone. I swam out and carried you to shore."

She opened her mouth to speak but said nothing. She studied the young man before her, focusing on his heavy sweater and cloddy brown boots.

"I'm sorry," Key added softly.

Finally the girl's expression changed. She straightened her shoulders and brushed the hair out of her eyes. The color had returned to her cheeks since he saw her last, and Key could see a certain fire lurking in her delicate face.

"You...you are the one who pulled me from the water?" she asked, and not only was Key taken aback by her sudden words, but by her accent- she sounded so different from the people of Graystone Island!

"Yes," Key answered. He did not have a chance to complete his thoughts because the girl lashed out and struck him across the face. He almost stumbled backward because he had not expected such a reaction from her. He usually knew when his father was going to hit him, but this blow took him by surprise.

"I didn't need you to save me!" she snapped. "Why didn't you just let me die?"

"What do you mean?" Key cried. "I couldn't let you die!"

"My mother and father were on that boat!" she yelled. " *They were all I had!* I should've gone with them. Don't you get it? *I should've died, too!*"

Key creased his brow and rubbed his sore cheek. His hope for redemption was fading.

"Wait a minute," Key suddenly remembered. "*You* called to *me*. You *asked* me to help you out on that rock."

The girl's expression softened. She turned her back on the young man who saved her, staring out the office window. The gray afternoon sky was a swirl of dark clouds, spreading shadows across the ocean. Black rocks and stones surrounded the doctor's cottage, coming to rest beneath the office window.

"Why is there no color here?" she said quietly, not really expecting an answer. Key stood behind her, wanting to say the right words, wishing he could take her pain away.

"I'm sorry," he said again, "for everything. I know what you must be going through."

"Do you?" she asked sarcastically. When he did not answer, she simply said, "Leave me alone."

Key nodded. "I'll be back again tomorrow."

"I don't care."

"Well, I do," he replied. "I'll see you soon."

And then he was gone, and the survivor was left alone to contemplate her arrival in a strange, empty, colorless new world.

CHAPTER 5

"There goes Lorn Terek's son," a voice whispered in the street. *"He brought that foreigner here."*

Key turned to find the source of the voice, but all he saw were eyes- villagers staring at him and whispering. He had been fishing all morning in the frigid Baric waters for their food.

"Would put me to shame if he were my son," another voice said.

Key walked down the gray cobblestone street with the morning's catches draped over his shoulder. His arm ached beneath the weight of the heavy fish, so he hoped he would reach the market soon. He was not surprised by the reaction of the islanders. They were a skeptical, superstitious bunch; fiercely loyal to his father. Word always traveled quickly among them, so he was prepared for their behavior.

"Hallo, Key!" Jackie Aldridge called from the seamstress' doorway. "Been to see the Kind Doctor lately?"

"Yes, Jackie," Key called back. "Saw him yesterday as a matter of fact. I'll tell him you asked."

Key continued to walk through town, past the fountain that never sprayed water, across the cracking stone courtyard, nodding to passerby and smiling at all who looked his way.

"Say there, Key," Johnson Laridae called from the window of Laridae's Tavern. "That's quite a catch ya got there!"

"Sure is, Mr. Laridae! The terns spotted a whole school of codfish near the shore this morning," Key responded, knowing full-well that the tavern keeper cared little about fishing.

"Is'at so?" Laridae chuckled. "Might want to take some down to the Kind Doctor's place then, since he's got an extra mouth to feed these days."

Key nodded, concealing his anger, heading straight to the market and never looking back.

***

By the time Key reached the market, his head was filled with insults and comments. Voices trailed behind him, whispering about the 'bad omen that Key Terek dragged ashore.' No one dared to say these things to his face because his father was so well-respected, but Key heard each and every word. Nothing could ever make him change his mind about the survivor. He was driven by an inner voice that begged for redemption and longed for light to fall across the sea again.

And, of course, there was the girl. He saw her face in his dreams that night, but he could not make out what she was saying. He just remembered her eyes, filled with pain and sadness, haunting him in his sleep. He even thought about her while he fished that morning, hearing her cries mingled with the strange calls of the sea birds.

Key Terek had grown up in a frigid black tower, on an island with prejudiced people who cared only for themselves and their kind. Samuel and Nanny provided friendship, but they could not fill the emptiness he felt inside. Part of Key believed that the emptiness was supposed to be there, while still another part of him- an unknown, subconscious part- sought to fill it. This, along with the hope for redemption, was what sent him back to visit the shipwreck girl, even after hearing the array of island gossip, even after she had sent him away the day before. He was not going to give up on her.

***

Key found her once again sitting on the stone floor in the doctor's office, head leaning against the wall.

"Does she sleep there?" Key whispered to the doctor. "On the floor?"

The doctor shook his head. "We offered her the couch but she refuses to leave the office. She hasn't moved much."

"Has she told you her name yet?" Key asked.

"No," the doctor replied. "She won't talk to us at all."

" I can hear you," the survivor suddenly snapped. "I'm not deaf."

Key raised an eyebrow and smiled. The doctor left them alone and Key approached her the same way he did the day before.

Her skin was much darker than Key's, and her cheeks were rosy from the sun. She did not resemble the citizens of Graystone Island, that much was certain. Her eyes, a soft shade of velvety brown, remained locked on him as he approached.

"You really should get up," Key suggested. "The floor must be cold."

"I'll sit where I please," the girl snapped.

"Okay," Key shrugged.

"Why are you here?" she asked.

"I told you I would be back."

"And I told you I didn't care."

Key bent down to her level, and as he did so, his old sketchbook tumbled from his sweater pocket. He reached out to grab it, but quick as a minnow, she snatched it up. He tried to take it from her hands but she stood up and brought it closer to the window light, leafing through the wrinkled pages.

"What is this?" she asked. "Did you draw these?" She flipped through the pages, touching some of the sketches, running her fingers along the dark lines.

"Yes, although not many lately. I carry the book with me out of habit. I drew most of the pictures when I was young."

She looked him up and down. "You're still young."

"Younger than I am now," he corrected.

"Are these all from your island?"

"Yes," he replied, sitting down in the doctor's wooden chair. "I've never been anywhere else."

"I've seen these at sea," she said, stopping at a sketch of the puffins. "Out in the middle of the ocean, with no land for miles. They can swim."

"Yes, they only spend part of the year on our island. The rest of the time they hunt at sea."

"Seems like an odd life."

"Maybe," Key said. "I was always jealous of them."

She eyed him warily and tossed the sketchbook back, but Key failed to catch it and it fell to the floor. He slid down next to her and picked it up.

"You're a good artist," she said.

He shrugged, staring down at his own wrinkled artwork. "Thanks."

"I'm sorry I hit you," she said flatly.

"It's okay, I'm used to it," Key replied. She looked confused, so he changed the subject and pointed to the dress that was peeking out from beneath the woolen blanket. "That's pretty."

He reached out and touched the edge of her dress. It was soft and silky between his fingers, so unlike the scratchy wool they wore on Graystone. And the colors! Swirls of purple, red, yellow, and orange. "I've never seen anything like this," Key marveled.

The girl snatched the dress from his hand. "It's from home," she said, and her eyes welled with tears.

"Where is home?" Key asked hesitantly. "Where are you from?"

"The Green Islands," she said, and Key thought he had heard her wrong.

It's impossible to reach The Green Islands, they are thousands of miles away, Lorn's voice echoed in his head.

Impossible.

But now this girl was *here*, sitting before Key with colorful clothes and skin like pure sunlight.

"Are you really from The Green Islands?" he asked. "If that's true, then how did you get..." he paused before continuing, not even wanting to mention his home, "...*here*?"

The girl laughed bitterly. "You dragged me ashore."

"No, I mean, why did you leave there? Why on earth would you leave?"

It took the girl several moments to respond, and when she did, her voice was distant and cold. "I was sailing around the world with my parents. We wanted to see places we had never seen before." She paused, biting her bottom lip. She stared blankly ahead, eyes wide.

"My father grew up on a boat, living near a lagoon...how could we crash? He knew everything about the sea." She shook her head as tears dripped down her cheeks.

It wasn't his fault, Key wanted to say, but he kept quiet.

"I was awake, I was standing there on the deck," the girl muttered, wiping her cheeks with the back of her hand. "The fog was thick, but there was no light, no foghorn. We saw nothing. This island wasn't here. As far as I'm concerned it just *wasn't here*. And then the rocks were cutting everything apart. I couldn't see, it was so cold..."

She continued to shake her head in astonishment, re-playing the accident in her mind. Key opened his mouth to explain, but couldn't find the words. "I'm sorry," was all he could muster.

"I just can't believe they're gone," she said.

Key touched her shoulder gently and the girl did not push him away. She closed her eyes and cried.

"You're not alone," Key reassured her. "You might not want us, but we're here to help. The Kind Doctor and Nanny are good people. And me, my name's Key."

The girl remained silent, her eyes closed. His hand was still resting on her shoulder so he gave her a little squeeze for comfort.

"Do you have a name?" he asked, raising his eyebrows inquisitively.

It seemed like an eternity before she answered, but when she did, her voice was loud and strong.

"Aurora," she said, opening her eyes. "My name is Au-rora Laelia."

CHAPTER 6

The puffins huddled together on the black rocks, focusing their little red eyes towards land. They were there when the foreign ship sank out at sea, and they were there when the young fisherman pulled a mysterious girl from the water. The puffins had seen numerous shipwrecks over the years, but never any survivors. They were used to darkness on their rocky shores, but they could sense a change in the air. They had nested on Graystone Island for hundreds of years, producing generations of pufflings who witnessed all that occurred around them. They could feel change coming like a storm approaching from the west.

Key smiled at the clown-like puffins as he sketched. He hadn't drawn in his notebook for many years, but felt inspired to fill the blank pages again. His hand moved quickly back and forth, trying to capture the puffins on paper. Their brightly colored beaks and button eyes always reminded him of how strange and unpredictable life could be.

Aurora. So now he knew her name. And it was a beautiful name. A foreign name. It made him think of light and color and faraway places. He visited her every day for two weeks straight. It was a slow process, but she was healing. She was finally accepting Sam and Nanny's kindness, and she didn't throw food at the walls anymore. Some days she even smiled at Key, flashing him a shy grin that warmed his heart. But then the smile would fade, and sadness would wash over her again. Key tucked the notebook into his pocket and walked up the stone path to the Kind Doctor's cottage. He knew about grief and how it lingered, resurfacing to pull you under when you least expected it. He wanted to give her time.

Nanny opened the door as usual when Key rang the bell, pulling him inside by the shirt sleeve.

"She's doing much better today!" Nanny beamed. "Didn't cry at all this morning, and she even thanked Samuel before he left on house call."

"That's great news," Key smiled. But when they entered the Kind Doctor's office, Aurora was nowhere to be found.

"She was here just a minute ago," Nanny gasped. "I brought her lunch myself."

They searched the cottage to no avail. Nanny opened the front door and called Aurora's name, but there was only wind and crashing waves. Key walked around the outside of the cottage, scanning the landscape. His first thought was that his father had done something to her-taken her, hidden her, *killed* her.

But then a flash of color caught his eye in the distance. Aurora stood on the bluff, staring at the sea, her exotic island dress blowing around her ankles in the Baric wind. A gray woolen blanket was wrapped tightly around her shoulders and she clutched it to her chin for warmth. Key thanked Nanny and sprinted away from the cottage, past the puffins and across the rocks to Aurora.

***

Aurora stood very still on the edge of the bluff, watching the strange birds that dotted the rocks before her. Key knew that she sensed him coming, so he slowed his pace and waited for her to speak. The wind whipped her long brown hair across her back. She did not look at him but spoke loudly into the wind so he could hear.

"They're laughing," she stated.

Key looked around, but they were alone. "Who?"

"Those birds," she said, motioning her head towards the puffins.

Key stepped closer towards her. He knew every sea bird in the Baric. All of them had distinct, piercing cries or familiar sea calls. But puffins made a vocalization that sounded oddly like laughter.

"It does sound like that," Key agreed.

"I don't find anything funny here," Aurora said, turning to look at him. "Everything looks sad and it feels cold enough to freeze my blood."

"It won't," Key replied. "Although it feels like it."

"I don't belong here."

Key took off his heavy sweater and handed it to her. "Here, put this on. It will help."

She hesitated but snatched the sweater away from him, letting the scratchy woolen blanket fall to her feet. Her colorful island dress was revealed in all of its splendor now- a long, flowing piece of fabric that danced around her ankles. Even torn from the wreck, it was shimmery and beautiful. She was wearing a pair of Nanny's boots with no socks and it made Key smile.

"Thank you," she said. Her teeth chattered from the cold air. "I'm not used to this."

Key nodded. "I suppose it's much warmer where you're from."

"Yes, and the sun always shines and the sky is blue. Not like this place."

Key tossed a stone over the edge of the bluff. He was glad she could not see the Darkhouse from where she was standing.

"I'm ready to go home now," she said. "I mean, I don't have any money, but I can work- is there a town? I can earn my keep for a small boat, maybe head towards The Blue Coast. That's not far from here, right?

Key opened his mouth to speak but was at a loss for words.

"If I can't buy a boat, I can hire a captain. Maybe Sam and Nanny will let me stay with them until I can earn some money to leave."

"Aurora," Key said softly, "You can't leave."

She glared at him. "What do you mean?"

"We don't have boats here," Key explained. She started to protest but he spoke over her, knowing what she was going to say. "We have no boats and no boats come here."

"That's ridiculous!" she exclaimed. "Where do you get your clothing, your food?"

"Everything we have comes from the island," Key said. "We used to receive trade shipments, but that was a long time ago. No one comes here anymore."

He did not go into further detail, but he was aching to explain. He did not tell her about his father or the day the trade ships stopped coming. He certainly did not tell her about the Darkhouse.

"So you're saying I'm stranded here?"

"I'm sorry," he repeated. "but yes."

"Gravestone," she said in a detached voice. "Is that what you call this place?"

"*Gray*stone," Key corrected. "I know it feels like a gravestone sometimes. Like a giant tomb."

Aurora began to cry and collapsed on the bluff in a sobbing heap. She covered her face in her hands, wanting to block out the tears. Key knelt down beside her.

"I'm sorry!" he pleaded, "I am so sorry! I want to make everything right for you-"

"But it's never going to be right!" she snapped. "Don't you understand that? This island that you call your tomb is now *my* tomb! *I don't want to die here like my parents!*"

Key lowered his head, searching for something to say, but his mind was blank. The puffins watched them cautiously, alarmed by the shouting. Aurora wiped her tears away.

"There's got to be a way off this island," she said.

"There isn't."

"There has to be."

"Don't you think I've tried?"

"Maybe you didn't try hard enough!" she yelled, and her voice echoed across the bluff.

"When I was twelve I tried to build a boat. It cracked to pieces on the rocks and I almost drowned. When I was thirteen I swam out as far as I could to see if I could spot any trace of land beyond Graystone. The water was so cold that I got hypothermia and almost drowned. When I was fourteen I built another boat and tried to launch from the north side of the island. The rocks sheared the bottom of my boat clean off and *I almost drowned.* Your ship crashed on our rocks and your *parents* drowned! *You* almost *drowned! Do you see the pattern here?"*

Key didn't tell her everything. He left out more planned attempts, more failures, and of course, he left out the punishments he received from his father, each and every time.

A wave of guilt and anger washed over Aurora. Despite what she told him, she remembered the fear out at sea and hanging onto the slippery black rock. She remembered calling for help, thinking no one could possibly hear her. Somewhere deep inside, she was grateful.

"I blame you because there is no one else to blame," she said. "But it's not your fault."

"I don't know how to help you cope with this," Key responded. "Maybe becoming friends is a start."

"I could use a friend," she said. "I could use a friend who *helps*. Friends solve problems together, right?"

"And Sam and Nanny are your friends," Key added.

"Do they know how to build a boat?" she asked. "Maybe they can help, too."

"No," Key answered. "Do *you* know how to build a boat?"

"No," she said quietly. "But I've seen others build them. I can make repairs. I can sew."

Key felt a glimmer of hope spark inside of him, but it quickly faded. There weren't enough supplies to build a boat on Graystone Island. He had tried so many times.

"I'm not giving up," Aurora added, reading his expression. "I don't care what you say. There has to be a way off this island and I am going to find it."

Until Lorn stops you, Key thought. *He always does.*

CHAPTER 7

A qua blue waves lapped against the sandy white shores. Tall, green palm trees stretched into the sky, waving their leaves in the warm ocean breeze. The sky was aglow with a heavenly sunset; shades of pink, orange and lavender melted across the horizon. Aurora was home, running along the beaches of The Green Islands, laughing in the wind. She caught sight of an odd little bird sitting near the shore. It looked back at her with button red eyes and a colorful, curved beak. A puffin? On The Green Islands? Aurora glanced behind her and there were puffins everywhere- in the trees, on the sand, in the water. All at once they chattered to one another- a deep, honking chortle that sounded like laughter. Aurora ran to escape the sound, but the wet sand slowed her down. She tripped and fell over a piece of driftwood, landing at the feet of a huge black puffin. 'You can't go home, Aurora,' the puffin croaked. It opened its brightly colored beak and laughed, grunting and snorting at her.

"No!" Aurora sat up with a start, only to be greeted by darkness in the Kind Doctor's living room. She pulled the blankets closer to her chest and fell back against the sofa pillows. She glanced around the empty room, half-expecting a puffin to spring out from beneath the table.

Aurora stood up in the darkness and glanced at the wooden clock on the mantelpiece. It was 4:30am, black as pitch on the island of Graystone. A fire was still burning in the fireplace, but the light was dying, so she poked at it and tossed another log in, watching the flames glow brighter. A puff of warm air touched her face, reminding her of The Green Islands. She closed her eyes and tried to picture home.

A knock on the window startled her into reality and the images of home quickly vanished. She gasped when she saw a shadowy figure outside, waving to her.

She cautiously approached the window and realized that the figure was Key, staring back at her through the glass. Her breath fogged over the image of his face and she wiped it away. He smiled in the darkness and motioned for her to open the window.

"What are you doing here?" she whispered.

"I'm heading out to fish," he whispered back. "I noticed the firelight and I just wanted to make sure you were okay."

"I'm fine," she assured him, then raised an eyebrow inquisitively. "You fish in the dark?"

"I get the traps and nets ready," he explained. "It takes a while."

She peered out the window and saw all of the equipment he was dragging- nets, hooks, a bucket filled with tools.

"Want to come with me?" Key asked. "I'll show you what I do."

Aurora wasn't sure if she wanted to know, but she was eager to erase the upsetting nightmare and clear her head.

"Yes!" she exclaimed, quickly closing the window.

She still had the sweater he had given her, so she snatched it off the sofa, slipped on a pair of boots, and headed out the door to catch up with the young fisherman who had saved her from the sea.

***

"It's so dark," Aurora whispered to Key as she followed him along the pebbly beach. "How can you see what you're doing?"

They reached a level section of shoreline and Key dropped his equipment. He crouched beside her and unraveled his nets.

"You get used to it," he said. "Why are you whispering?"

"I don't know- because it's dark?" Aurora replied, still whispering.

Key laughed. "I'd be whispering all the time, then. This island is always dark."

Aurora chuckled in return. She watched as Key carefully tied hooks to each pole, then leaned them against y-shaped stands along the shore. The work was tedious in the darkness, and by the time he was finished, there were dozens of baited rods along the beach. Then he gathered the loose nets that he had stored between the rocks, slinging them over his back.

"I don't use these till the birds show me where to go," he explained.

"The puffins?" she asked.

"No," Key answered. "Usually the shearwaters or some other diving birds. The puffins swim far out for their food so it's harder for me to see where they're hunting. They prefer a certain type of fish, too, not a villager favorite. The shearwaters fly low over the best fishing spots. They're very smart."

"Where are they now?" Aurora asked.

"Resting," Key said with a smile. "They'll be up with the light."

Aurora was beginning to wonder if the sun would ever rise. The darkness seemed so permanent on Graystone Island, so content without the sun. But sure enough, after Key had prepared all of his fishing gear and set out his lines, the sky began to lighten, very slowly. Aurora was waiting patiently for a sunrise. She was eager to see pastel colors spread across the sky and birds float through the morning air like butterflies. But that wasn't quite how it happened. The sky went from black, to a lighter shade of black, to dark gray, then light gray. Aurora could not even see the sun, let alone feel it. The sky was just a washed-out haze, drained of color. The birds did appear- scroungy looking shearwaters with ruffled gray backs, giant petrels flapping their long, curved wings, and seagulls screaming for their mates. To Aurora, these birds were frightening and ugly. They were weather-beaten creatures, intent on finding food. She sat beside Key, watching them warily as they soared through the sky.

Key followed the birds as they flew, springing from rock to rock with his nets, waiting for the perfect moment to toss them into the sea. To him, these birds were beautiful and graceful. He was grateful to them because they taught him where to fish, and he envied them for being able to fly high into the sky, away from Graystone Island.

"I had a job, too," Aurora suddenly said.

"You did?" Key asked. "What did you do?"

"Well, it wasn't a job that was assigned to me or anything. Not like here."

"How did you know my job was assigned to me?"

"Nanny told me," Aurora answered. "My job was fun. I worked on my grandmother's orchid farm."

Key gasped. "I've never seen an orchid."

"They're beautiful," Aurora said. "and kind of fragile."

"What did you do there?"

"I helped to care for the orchids. Sometimes I helped the customers who visited. My grandmother grew the most beautiful orchids in all of The Green Islands. We had to sell the farm when she passed away. It was a hard time."

"I'm sorry," Key said. "Is that why you left?"

Aurora shrugged. "We left because we needed a change. I needed a change."

"I can certainly understand that."

"All of that beauty and I wasn't happy," Aurora added. "It seems ridiculous now."

"It's not ridiculous," Key said. "I think it takes work to be happy."

Aurora watched Key dunk his arms into the cold water, set up nets and cast baited hooks. His sleeves were pushed up over his elbows, and Aurora noticed trails of red scars along both forearms.

"What happened to you?" she asked, pointing to the scars.

Key looked at her, searching for the correct way to answer. He pulled his sleeves back down to hide his wounds. He wasn't sure if she would understand.

Aurora knew what it felt like to be overwhelmed with sadness. She knew how heavy depression could be and how it could take over, leaving such hopelessness. Her heart ached for him.

"Sometimes," he began cautiously, "during certain seasons, there are no fish. The water is either too cold, or the birds too hungry, and there aren't any fish close to shore. I don't have a boat so there's no way for me to follow the schools."

Aurora remained quiet, listening intently, so Key took a deep breath and continued.

"I have to lure the fish to shore," he explained, "especially the big ones. They can feed more people on this island. I'm supposed to use chum, or blood of some kind to bring them here. The easiest bait would be the birds, but I refuse to kill the creatures that help me fish. Plus, the puffins are kind of sacred here - it's a bad omen to kill them."

"That's not at all what I thought you were going to say," she replied, confused. "But, wait, what *are* you saying?"

"I am the bait," he explained. "I cut my arms when fish are scarce and mix the blood with whatever else I have for bait- food scraps, leftover whale oil from the trade days. I spread that in the ocean until it attracts bigger fish."

Aurora knew that he couldn't possibly attract many fish by mutilating himself, yet still he did this to supply his island with food.

"I thought you might have tried to- you know-"

"What? No!" Key gasped. "I may hate it here but I try not to let that kind of darkness pull me under. There are beautiful things here and I focus on that-the birds, the sea- I like the quiet. I look for those good things. At least, I try to. Like I said, it takes work to be happy."

"Do you have friends here?"

"None my age. They don't...understand me. Sam and Nanny are my friends, and that's enough for me."

"They seem like good people," Aurora agreed.

"Do you have friends?" Key asked. "At your home, I mean."

"Not really," Aurora said without hesitation. "I was always the one who didn't get invited; the one who was left out. My mother used to say I was too much for people."

"Too much?" Key looked up from his nets and smiled. "I find that hard to believe."

"Your parents," Aurora began, "do they worry about you carving yourself up for the sake of others?"

"I choose to fish this way," Key said defensively. "My father doesn't care, and my mother died long before I started fishing."

"I'm sorry," Aurora apologized. "I didn't mean to upset you."

Key shrugged. "You're right, my mother would probably disapprove of my fishing methods. She cared a lot about me. My father, well, he's a different story."

"Why?" Aurora asked.

Key shrugged. "He's cruel. I don't know what my mother ever saw in him. She said he wasn't always mean and that he took care of her. She said he helped her when she needed him. I never saw that side of him. He was always mean, and it got worse over time."

Aurora lowered her head sadly. Key continued to work as he spoke, reeling in fish and dumping them in buckets, tying bait to hooks and casting new lines, over and over again.

"My mother named me Key because she said I would be the key to my father's heart. I don't know why she believed that. I was not the key to his heart. I am not the key to anyone's heart. My name is pointless."

"Maybe things will change." Aurora suggested. "Maybe he will change."

"*Him*?" Key laughed bitterly. "That will never happen. He'll just stay in that wretched Darkhouse for the rest of his pathetic life."

"Dark house?" Aurora repeated. "What dark house?"

All at once, Key realized what he had said, and he couldn't take it back.

"There are some things I haven't told you about this island," he said.

"Like what?" Aurora could feel her stomach drop.

"My father, Lorn, runs this island. Many years ago he was the lighthouse keeper and overseer of all trade ships. But things changed and he didn't want foreign ships on our shores anymore. He convinced the islanders that we needed to preserve our heritage and keep others out, which was actually pretty easy because our entire island is surrounded by sharp rocks. He removed our one trade dock - tore the whole thing down. He burned any remaining boats. He painted the lighthouse black and extinguished it."

Aurora's eyes widened.

"That's why we didn't see the island," she gasped. "My father knew how to sail, he knew how to navigate; he didn't steer away from this place because *he couldn't see it!*"

"I told you my father is cruel," he said.

"Cruel? That's not just cruelty, that's murder!" she cried. "How many ships have crashed? We weren't the first?"

"No," Key said, "You were not the first."

Aurora was speechless.

"Most trade ships knew to stop coming - word of mouth, I guess," Key continued. "They knew they couldn't dock here safely anymore. But travelers-"

"Like my family?" Aurora interrupted. "Innocent mariners with no clue of this island's existence! How many people died, Key? How many boats were lost?"

"I don't know," he said softly.

Some of the fishing lines were tugging lightly across the shore, but he ignored them.

"Does your father know these boats crashed? That people died?"

"He doesn't care."

"And the villagers?"

"They think the loss is necessary to preserve their heritage," Key answered.

"Sam and Nanny? They believe this, too?"

"They are afraid of my father. What can they possibly do?"

Tears of anger formed in Aurora's eyes but she blinked them back and clenched her fists.

"Where is this Darkhouse?"

"That way," Key pointed, "across town. It overlooks everything."

She pushed past him and climbed down the black rocks, calling back to him as she went.

"We'll see about this Darkhouse! We'll see what your father has to say to me!"

"Aurora, don't!" Key cried.

He abandoned his fishing gear and ran after her. She was walking fast with clenched fists, heading straight towards town. He called her name several more times but she ignored him. There was nothing he could do but follow.

CHAPTER 8

It was almost noon when Aurora reached the edge of town, and when the villagers caught sight of her, they stopped and stared.

She was wearing Key's navy blue sweater over her colorful floral print dress, its hem waving in the breeze. She met no eyes as she marched through the center of town, even though everyone gaped openly at her.

"Would you look at that lassie," one of the villagers snickered. "thinks she's some kind of island princess."

Other calls and whispers followed, but Aurora blocked them out. She kept her eyes focused on the Darkhouse in the distance.

"Where is *she* off to in such a hurry?" someone said.

"What nerve she has, showing herself in town like that."

"She's the one Key Terek has taken a fancy to, imagine that."

"Too bad she can't go back where she came from."

Aurora wished she *could* go back where she came from. As she marched past gawking islanders and gossiping ladies, she cursed them under her breath, wishing she could see the smiling faces of the Green Islanders again.

Aurora's thoughts were interrupted the moment she caught sight of the Darkhouse. It reached high into the sky at the edge of town, looming over the village like a threatening black shadow. No light shined from its windows. It was silent and dark, and Aurora felt cold just looking at it. A small cottage sat at the base of the Darkhouse. There was a narrow, ash-covered smokestack on its thatched roof, and a plume of dark gray smoke curled from the top.

The wind howled around Aurora's ears, as if warning her of the danger within. But she pressed on, driven by anger, and rang the cottage bell furiously. From the corner of her eye she saw Key coming up the path beside her, but he stopped several feet away. She rang the bell again.

"LORN TEREK!" she screamed at the door. "LORN TEREK, show yourself!"

***

Lorn Terek was still asleep in his bed when the voice reached his ears. He snorted and sniffed out of his dreamless slumber, thinking it was the voice of his dead wife, calling to him from the grave. He rolled out of bed with a grunt, scratching his stomach and belching loudly.

"Mariana? Is'at you?" he muttered.

Lorn was a huge, burly man with a hairy black chest and balding head. He stood well over six feet tall with a protruding belly that hung over his pants. The ground shook when he walked, and people knew to get out of his way on most occasions. No one ever said no to Lorn Terek. No one dared to cross his path or challenge his reasoning. So when he heard that voice calling his name, he assumed he was dreaming, because Mariana Terek wouldn't even dare to haunt him.

***

Aurora stood before the Darkhouse cottage, waiting. The black tower took on its own persona against the gray sky, and it stood there watching her with malice.

"Lorn Terek!" Aurora screamed again. "Lorn Terek, I know you're in there!"

It took a long time for Lorn Terek to get out of bed, and the voice was angering him now. He struggled with his robe, shoving his arms through the sleeves as he approached the door. He neglected to tie the sash, leaving his hairy belly exposed.

"What is the meaning of this?" Lorn shouted as he whipped the door open. When he caught sight of Aurora on his doorstep, he sneered with disgust. "*Green girl!* Get off my property!"

Aurora responded by slapping him in the face. From somewhere behind her, Key let out an audible gasp.

"You killed my family!" she cried.

Lorn pushed her away with one large hand, and she stumbled backwards onto the stone pathway.

"How dare you strike me!" he shouted, looming over her. "You are not welcome here, Green girl!"

"You killed them," Aurora said, struggling to her feet. Key leaned down timidly and helped her up. "You killed my parents!"

"I don't know what you're talking about!" he snapped. "I am not to blame for your navigational skills."

"There was no light to guide us!" she yelled. "It is *your* fault that there was no light to guide our ship!"

She lunged at him again, unable to control her emotions, but he grabbed her by the neck, lifting her slightly off the ground. Her feet momentarily kicked in the air and she clawed at his hand, unable to breathe.

"Father, no!" Key pleaded, grabbing Lorn by the forearm. Lorn tightened his grip and Aurora's face turned red.

"Who do you think you are, coming here and accusing me like this?" Lorn spoke through clenched teeth, squeezing harder. "You don't belong here, girl. We have no room for you."

He released his grip and threw her to the ground where she lay gasping for air, choking and wheezing.

"You...brought me here..." she gasped. "I can't...leave..."

"*He* brought you here! Not me!" Lorn yelled, pointing at Key. "And don't you forget that!"

Key hung his head but said nothing. Aurora rubbed at her neck and tried to clear her throat.

"My parents were good people," she continued. "You killed them with your Darkhouse."

"*Enough!*" Lorn snapped, marching towards her again, threatening to strike. "You shut your mouth, *now*, girl, or I'll shut it for you! If you were a villager, you would be punished by now, your words silenced-"

"*But I am not a villager!*" Aurora managed to cry out. "And if you resent my presence here then blame yourself, for it was *you* who led me here and *you* who stranded me here!"

"Get out of my sight before I make you disappear."

Key helped Aurora to her feet and tried to pull her away, frightened of what Lorn might do next if they remained.

"You put me to shame, boy!" Lorn yelled to Key. "Don't come back to this house! *Don't ever come back here!*"

He threw a large stone in their direction and it hit Key in the back. Aurora gasped in outrage and turned towards Lorn, but Key grabbed her by the hand. She pulled her hand away and struggled again to turn back.

"Don't," he urged. "It's not worth it."

Key gently touched her shoulder, steering her away from Lorn and the Darkhouse. He just wanted to be far, far away. He could feel her trembling and the palms of her hands were bleeding. Although she seemed physically defeated, she managed to turn around one last time to release a string of profanities in Lorn's direction.

***

"Why is my voice so raspy?" Aurora asked the Kind Doctor, touching her neck.

"Your windpipe is bruised," Samuel explained. "It might take a little while but it will go back to normal. Drink a lot of water and try to speak in a soft tone."

"What about her eye?" Key asked.

"The broken blood vessel in her eye will dissipate. Just give it time."

Nanny handed her a jar of ointment. "Rub this on those bruises and you'll heal up in no time," she smiled, motioning towards Aurora's neck.

Aurora took the ointment and stared at it in bewilderment. "So that's it? That's all we do? We patch up wounds and sweep it all under the rug?"

"There is nothing we can do, Aurora," Samuel said.

"Nothing you can do? Are you serious?"

"We have no strength against Lorn," Nanny explained. "We just keep our distance, keep to ourselves."

"If you turn a blind eye then you are part of the problem!" Aurora snapped.

"Aurora-" Key began.

"No, it's true," she said, cutting him off. "You let a madman make decisions for you. There is strength in numbers. You could rise up against him."

"Rise up? Two old folk and a boy?" Key said. "And then what? We don't have any weapons. We don't know how to run an island or a lighthouse."

"Then your complacency will be the death of you!"

She stormed out of the Kind Doctor's cottage and ran. She didn't know where she was running to but she needed to run far and fast.

CHAPTER 9

Aurora had been trapped on Graystone Island for almost forty days. In that time, she had only explored a few parts of the island, and so far it all looked the same. But as she ran away from the cottage, she found herself in new territory. There were trees here- still dark in color but green nonetheless- tall, thin pines with scrawny branches. Yellow tufts of grass sprouted beside the trees, dry and coarse to the touch. The ground sloped upwards, so she walked higher until she came to a clearing that overlooked most of the island. She could see the Darkhouse off in the distance, looming quietly over the village. She brushed past the trees and accidentally disturbed some starlings that were taking refuge in the branches. Suddenly she noticed two small mounds of earth, heaped neatly on the ground by her feet. Crosses made of branches sat before them, adorned with shiny white seashells tied to burlap strings. Aurora walked further past the trees and saw another mound, this one older, since the yellow grass had grown over it and the cross looked weathered. There were no seashells tied to this cross but there was a smooth, heart-shaped stone at its base. A thumping sound interrupted her thoughts as Key bounded through the trees, out of breath from trying to catch up to her. She was not surprised to see him since she heard him following the entire way.

"You sure can run," he said between breaths.

"And you sure are loud," she replied. "What is this place?"

"I call it the New Cemetery," he said. "It's not tradition to bury the dead on Graystone. The dead belong at sea. But my mother once told me about cemeteries and tombstones. And I needed a place," he paused. "A place where I could remember things."

"Things?" she asked. "Or people?"

"Both."

"We have cemeteries on the Green Islands," Aurora said. "Whose grave is this?" She pointed to the mound by her feet.

"That's my mother."

"And these?" she pointed to the newer graves behind him.

He looked at her, afraid to answer. "Those are your parents."

Aurora inhaled sharply and walked closer to the small piles of earth.

"There are no bodies," Key said. "I'm sorry, that didn't come out right. I just mean...I didn't...find them."

Aurora knelt beside the makeshift graves and touched each seashell, rolling them between her fingertips.

"I found some debris from the wreckage, just some scraps of metal and wood. That's what I buried. My mother liked seashells, so I used those, too."

"Why didn't you tell me?" she asked.

"I was going to, I just didn't know how."

"Why did you do this?"

Key wasn't exactly sure why, so he didn't reply. But she turned and looked at him, and her eyes demanded answers.

"I felt responsible. And I wondered if you would need a place to visit, too," he paused and lowered his head. "To remember things."

"I don't need a place to remember things," she said. "There's no way I could forget."

"I just felt like they should be at peace," Key explained.

Aurora wondered if her parents would ever be at peace. Her mother once told her that funerals were for the living, and that certainly made sense to her now. But she was touched by Key's gesture. She stood and walked over to him.

"Thank you," she said with tears in her eyes. Without hesitation, she reached out and threw her arms around him, hugging him tightly. Key could not remember the last time he was hugged this way, and for a moment he froze with his arms out straight, unable to respond. But then his heart took charge and he gingerly embraced her in return. They both started to cry, sobbing lightly into each other's shoulders.

"I can still see them, you know," Aurora said. "But it's different now. When I close my eyes, I don't see the bad things like the shipwreck and the water."

"No?"

"No. I see their faces," Aurora replied. "My mother's kind eyes. My father's bright smile. He would take me places where the water was as blue as the sky."

Her sentences trailed off into silence and she stood in the wind, still holding Key. There was only gray around her now, with various shades of black and white. There were no more blue skies or smiling parents.

"My mother's face is fading in my mind," Key said. "I can see her smile but her features are blurry. I worry that I won't remember her voice or the exact color of her hair."

"I worry about that, too," Aurora agreed. "How old were you when your mom died?"

"Eight," Key said. "I was eight. My mother was beautiful. Her name was Mariana."

His voice broke as he said her name aloud. Aurora knew this was fragile territory but she pressed on. She needed to know the truth.

"What happened to her?"

Key shook his head and refused to answer, but Aurora looked him in the eyes.

"Key," she urged, holding his shoulders with both hands. "I need you to tell me what happened to her."

Key immediately broke down sobbing. Embarrassed, he tried to hide his face.

"Key, what *happened* to her? Why can't you talk about it?"

Key sat in the dry grass and held his head in his hands. From somewhere far away he heard the puffins chortling on the rocks.

"She left us," Key said. "Lorn told everyone that she abandoned us- boarded a boat and left us behind." He took a deep breath and held back tears. "The villagers believed that she betrayed my father and left Graystone with a trader from the Blue Islands named London."

He punched his fist against his own head as if trying to extinguish the memory, and Aurora flinched. *"But that's not what happened at all,"* he added in a half-whisper.

Aurora knelt before him and held his hand. "You are my friend," she said. "And friends trust each other. You need to tell me what happened to her."

"Why?" Key cried. "Why does it matter anymore?"

"Because someone needs to hear the truth," Aurora said. "You need to say it out loud. *Tell me.*"

Key clenched his teeth. He took one deep breath and the words spilled out so quickly he couldn't stop them. "My father was always so mean, so angry all the time. He drank a lot and my mother was lonely. He hit her, he hit me- there was just so much anger, all the time. Eventually she befriended a trader from the Blue Coast named London Foster. He became her confidant and friend. I think they were in love and I didn't care. They tried to hide it from my father but everyone knew. She told me that she asked London for help and that he was going to get us off the island. I trusted him. He was like an uncle to me- he was the one who gave me the pencils and notebook that I use for my drawings. Lorn *hated* him." Key inhaled again and his breath shook. "One night she woke me up - it was midnight. She said to meet her outside and bring a change of clothes. I knew London was coming for us. But when I stepped outside that night, it was *so* dark. There was only one light coming from a lantern by the cliff. Lorn was there and he was arguing with my mother. Their backs were to me but I could hear them. Lorn had extinguished the beacon- the lighthouse was pitch black. My mother begged him to turn the light back on. It was so foggy that night, even thicker than usual."

Key wiped tears from his eyes. He didn't say anything more so Aurora tried to fill in the blanks.

"What happened to London?" she asked.

"The fog was so thick," Key paused and shook his head. His voice trailed off and tears stifled his voice. "It was so dark. There's no way he could find us, no way to maneuver through that-"

Aurora's heart sank as she remembered her own shipwreck- the fog, the darkness, the sharp, jagged rocks as the boat went under. Her heart broke over the loss of London, even though she never met him. Key tugged at the yellow grass by his feet, tearing out clumps and tossing it aside as he spoke.

"I hid. I hid behind a rock as soon as I saw my father. I was a coward."

"You were a child."

"I should have helped her. I should have tried to help London."

"What could you have done?" Aurora cried. "You were just a boy!"

"My mother was screaming at my father to turn the light back on. She must've been terrified for London."

"I'm sure she wanted to protect you, too."

"We had never seen the beacon go dark. The water looked strange without light. Everything was so ominous. My mother was beside herself, screaming and crying. Maybe Lorn was afraid the villagers would hear her. Maybe he was just angry-"

"What did he do?"

"My mother tried to run to the lighthouse but he grabbed her by the back of the hair," Key was sobbing now, he could barely speak. "She fell. She fell backwards and he kicked her. He kept kicking her, kicking her, over and over. And then before I knew it, he grabbed a rock and he held it over her head and...he hit her with it. He hit her in the face until she stopped moving."

Aurora was crying now, too, and she hugged him and held him tightly as he sobbed.

" I didn't do *anything!* I didn't help my mother, I didn't yell! I just watched him in the darkness like a coward. And then before I could even react, he dragged her to the cliff and...and...he pushed her...he pushed her off the cliff, into the water...like she was *nothing*, like she was worthless. I ran. He never saw me, so I ran back to the lighthouse and hid under my blankets. I didn't know where else to go. In the morning he told me she had left with London. He told everyone that. I knew it was a lie but I was too scared to say anything. After that he painted the lighthouse black- tore down the docks, abolished all trade. I never said a word. I was afraid he'd kill me, too.

"He probably would have," Aurora said softly. "You were just a boy. You're a victim, too, Key."

"I wasn't a victim! My mother was the victim, London was the victim. *Your parents* were victims. I was just a coward."

"No!" Aurora cried. "You were abused, don't you see that? Lorn is a murderer! An *abuser*. That's what abusers do! They control everything."

No one had ever called Key that before, *abused*. He never thought of himself as a victim. The word echoed in his head: *abused, abused, abused*. He didn't feel good about this new title, but deep down he knew it was true. Lorn had manipulated him, *abused* him. He was filled with sadness for recognizing it now and allowing it to go on for so long.

"I never thought of myself that way," Key said. "It makes me feel ashamed."

"You have nothing to be ashamed of. You're a survivor, like me. But in a different way."

They locked eyes and something in Key's stomach fluttered. They stood silently staring at each other, and something between them changed, like a light flickering in the darkness. He reached out and took her hand in his. Key waited for a reaction but Aurora did not pull her hand away like he thought she would. Instead, she squeezed his palm and smiled. But before he could say a word, a loud, melancholy sound broke through the air and Aurora jumped.

"What was *that*?" she asked nervously.

Key stared at the ocean. Off in the distance, a blue and white tail splashed the surface. A plume of water blew in the air with a loud "*pfshhhhh!*" Then the melancholy sound again.

"The whales are here!" Key exclaimed. "They only come a few times a year. They breed and hunt for fish. And they sing."

Aurora's eyes widened. "*Ohhhhh!*" she gasped. "So beautiful!"

Key pulled a small wooden device from his pocket. "Here," he said, handing it to her. "It's a spyglass. London gave it to me years ago."

Aurora peered through it and gasped again when the whales appeared closer in sight. She was grateful for the distraction and their calming presence. "We don't have whales like this in The Green Islands. *Oh!* I think there's a baby!"

She handed the spyglass to Key so he could see, too, and he smiled when he spotted the baby in the water. "That's the only place they can fish near the island," he said. "That's where our docks used to be. The water is deeper there and so are the rocks."

"But don't they eat all of your fish?"

"Not really. They like krill, mostly. There's enough for us to share."

He sat down in the grass and pulled out his sketchbook, quickly drawing the whale's tail. Then he drew the baby's small head poking through the waves.

"They sound like music," Aurora said. "I wish we could swim away with them."

That was the first time she had said *"we"* and Key noticed immediately. "Friends solve problems together, right?"

She looked at him and nodded. "Right."

There was a long, silent pause between them while Key continued to sketch. Then he lifted his head and looked her straight in the eyes.

"We need to get off this island."

"Yes we *do!!*" she cried, excited by his sudden spark of determination. She clapped her hands together, feeling proud.

So Key and Aurora sat on the clifftop, watching the whales and brainstorming ideas. Aurora drew a map in Key's sketchbook, or at least tried to. She only knew what her father had taught her. The map she drew showed The Green Islands, The Blue Coast, and The Central Reefs. She added some southern atolls they had visited, and a western archipelago they had noticed from a distance.

"The Blue Coast is the closest," Key said, lightly tapping her drawing. "That was where most of our trade came from."

"We need to build a boat," Aurora stressed. "Even if it's a small boat, we should be able to make it there. Maybe I can sew a sail."

Their plans felt huge- bigger than anything Key could contain in his mind. Everything he had ever tried in the past had failed. He had no real tools, only basic fishing supplies. Samuel had some minor equipment- a hammer, nails, screwdrivers, a saw. Everyone on Graystone Island had a purpose. There was a tavern keeper, a seamstress, a grocer, a carpenter, each with their own tools. But none would be willing to help Key and Aurora. If they attempted to purchase supplies from villagers, suspicion would arise. Every plan they devised seemed impossible. They brainstormed for so long that the sun began to set and the air grew even colder. The whales had long since vanished and Aurora shivered as the ocean breeze whipped across her face. Key's sketchbook was littered with new ideas, maps, and drawings of boats. He slipped it into his pocket and they headed down the hill.

CHAPTER 10

As Key and Aurora walked in silence, they heard another strange sound in the wind. It was a faint ringing of bells that reminded Aurora of home. It brought back warm memories of The Green Islands, and she pictured her mother's silver wind chimes hanging on the porch.

"Listen!" Key whispered, interrupting her thoughts. "Do you hear them?"

"Wind chimes?" Aurora questioned.

"The Elders!" Key replied in excitement. He grabbed her by the arm and pulled her aside so they wouldn't be seen. "Look there."

He pointed across the rocks to a line of dark figures moving slowly towards the village. Aurora watched them shuffle along single file, their hunched and crooked figures silhouetted against the moonlit sky. Each figure hobbled along with the aid of a walking stick, the largest one belonging to the caravan's leader. Bundles of tiny bells hung from his crutch, jingling with every step he took.

"What are they doing?" Aurora asked.

The Elders were small, aged people, yet Aurora found them intimidating. Their slow, methodical steps were unnerving, their moonlit shadows foreboding. She whispered to avoid being noticed by them.

"They're visiting relatives," Key explained. "I don't know which villager, but someone in town, I suppose, based on where they're walking."

"What do they want?'

"They're here to check up on their family, make sure they're adhering to island law. We have old traditions and people here are superstitious. Everyone wants to be blessed by their Elders. If your Elders are upset with you, it's a curse. You don't want to be cursed by your Elders."

"Why not?"

"Because it's like a mark of shame. People won't trust you. They won't want to deal with you or help you."

"What are your Elders like?"

"I never met them," Key said. "My father is always warning me about them but the last time they visited, I was an infant."

"Where do they live?"

"On the east side of the island. They all live in big, stone cottages near the cliffs. Some people say they keep puffins as pets."

Aurora pictured a puffin with a leash around its neck and the thought made her laugh out loud. The Elders stopped in their tracks and Key gasped. He quickly dropped to the ground and pulled Aurora down with him. The Elders continued shuffling along as Key and Aurora stifled their laughter. Aurora was laughing so hard that tears formed in the corners of her eyes. She hid her face against Key's shoulder to muffle her laughter.

Once the Elders were safely out of range, Key held out a hand and helped Aurora to her feet. Aurora took his hand and stood, stumbling slightly on the gravel. But when she tried to pull her hand away, he held her tighter.

"What?" she said in confusion.

Key didn't know what love was. He didn't understand the fluttery feeling in his stomach or why he couldn't stop thinking about Aurora. All he knew was that he didn't want to let go of her. He liked the feeling of her small hand in his. He liked being close to her and the soft feeling of her hair when it brushed his cheek. But he had no idea how to put those feelings into words.

"I'm glad you're here with me," was all he managed to say.

Aurora felt her heart quicken at his words, but she was careful with her own. She was glad to be with Key, too, but certainly not glad to be on Graystone Island.

"I don't think I ever thanked you," she said, afraid to meet his eyes. "for rescuing me, I mean."

"It's okay."

"No, it's not. You saved my life. I'm grateful for that. And the cemetery- that was really special."

Key blushed but Aurora could not see his reaction in the darkness. He squeezed her hand.

"*You're* really special," he added, finally looking her in the eyes.

The moment their eyes met, Aurora knew there was no turning back. She knew she could no longer hide what was bubbling inside of her. She tried to deny it but the feelings were there, bright and warm like sunlight. She leaned forward and pressed her mouth to his.

When their lips met, Key felt his heart leap. He knew this kiss was the beginning of everything. Emotions swirled inside of him, from love and passion to fear and regret. He was so happy to have found Aurora, to have saved her and brought her to the Kind Doctor's cottage. But he was sorry to have found her, too, trapping her on

Graystone like a prisoner. As they continued kissing in the shadowy darkness of the village, he knew their pact was sealed. They were a team now, and together they would find a way off Graystone Island once and for all. He wanted to love her far, far away, forever.

CHAPTER II

K ey stood on the foggy shore, yawning in the cold
morning air. He had stayed out well past sundown
with Aurora, and now he could barely keep his eyes open
while fishing. Several black-backed gulls circled near his
nets, crying loudly across the water. They swooped past his
head, cracking shellfish on the rocks.

Perhaps it was the antics of these seabirds or the drowsi-
ness in his veins that kept him from hearing footsteps
approaching in the distance. Whatever the reason, Key was
caught off guard when his father climbed down the rocks
and stood before him with a threatening scowl.

In all the years that Key had been fishing the Baric, not
once did his father offer to help. Never did Lorn Terek set
foot on the beaches where his son struggled with heavy
nets or broken fishing lines. Not even during the first year

of Key's fishing duties, when he was just a child, alone in the dark, frightened by the eerie sounds of the sea. His father had always remained locked away in the Darkhouse, snoring loudly or belching in his sleep.

Key did not say a word to his father. He continued baiting his hooks and tying lines without looking up.

"You are a disgrace," Lorn slurred, kicking the ground with his boots. "I have come all the way here to tell you that."

"I have work to do, father," Key said with a sigh, gathering up his net.

Lorn stepped on the net with one huge foot, and Key tugged at it in vain.

"Nothing is more important than what I have to say to you. Look at me when I speak to you, boy!"

Key let go of the net and stared up at his father, who stood towering over him like a storm cloud. Key rose to face him, determined not to falter.

"I was in Laridae's Tavern last night," Lorn began, pacing along the shore as he spoke. "I was enjoying my ale until Jackie Aldridge came through the door. *Lorn!* He said to me, *You'll never guess who I just saw out in the shadows!*"

Key remained quiet and stared at the sea. He said nothing, but inside he was crushed that someone had witnessed their most private, magical moment and shared it with Lorn.

"You have *disgraced* me, boy. It was bad enough that you pulled that trash from the sea, but *this*? This is inexcusable! I told you -*I told you*- to stay away from her! You were *seen in town* with that girl and now I'm a laughing stock- *a laughing stock!*"

"She's not trash!" Key snapped, kicking his net aside. "Don't you ever call her that again!"

Lorn's face contorted and he lashed out, punching Key in the stomach. Key doubled over, gasping for air.

"You're pathetic," Lorn snarled. "Get up! I'll teach you to speak to me that way! *Get up!*"

But Key could not get up. He knelt on the rocks, gasping as he tried to catch his breath. Lorn lashed out again, kicking Key in the ribs. Key's mind was a blur. He was lying on the ground, struggling to get to his feet and protect himself from Lorn's blows.

"Get up!" Lorn yelled again, grabbing Key by the sweater.

Lorn clenched Key's collar in one hand and punched Key in the face with the other. Key fell backwards on the rocks, hitting his head. Lorn leaned over, punching Key in the face over and over again. Blood poured from Key's nose and down the back of his throat, making him gag. He tried to yell "STOP" but only a horrible gurgling sound emerged.

"You will not see her again!" Lorn ordered as he stood over his bloody son. "If you do, that will be the end, Key. I swear to you, *that will be the end!*"

Lorn kicked Key in the ribs one last time, then stormed away, slurring profanities as he climbed over the rocks.

The terns circled high above, crying and screaming at the commotion. Key remained motionless on the shore, blood pooling beneath his head. Several gulls swooped close to him, brushing his face with their wingtips. But the young fisherman did not move.

CHAPTER 12

Someone was humming. Key heard it through the darkness- a soft, soothing song, calling him out of unconsciousness, welcoming him back to the world. He felt a soft hand stroking his cheek. It was this gentle kindness that nudged him from slumber, but searing agony that made him open his eyes.

Sharp pain clawed at his chest with every breath. The metallic taste of dried blood permeated his tongue, and he could feel that one of his back teeth was missing. His rib cage was bandaged tightly, and he could only take shallow, quick breaths without pain.

"Aurora?" Key said, trying to focus. One eye was swollen shut. He was not sure where he was, but he was certain that Aurora was beside him. It was her soft voice that roused him from darkness.

"I'm here," she whispered close to his ear. "You're in the Kind Doctor's office. We found you. It's all right now."

He squinted his one good eye and could see her face smiling down at him. He was aware of her hand in his, clutching his palm warmly, assuring him that he was safe- that *she* was safe.

"It's okay now," she said again. "Go to sleep. Go back to sleep. You need your rest."

It felt *so* good to rest. To not be worrying or working or struggling. Key nodded, calmed by Aurora's presence, and drifted into unconsciousness again. Aurora pressed his limp, bruised hand to her face and cried.

***

Key remained immobile for almost a week. For seven days he lay still while Samuel, Nanny and Aurora tended to him. Aurora's emotions rotated between anger and shame. They all knew Lorn was to blame for Key's condition, but they were too afraid to confront him. Aurora was ashamed of her fear. She had never been one to back down, never played the coward. But now she was trapped on an unfamiliar island far from home with no family to support her. The feeling of Lorn's hand squeezing the life from her neck still burned in her mind. So she assisted Samuel, tended to Key and kept quiet. She tried to come up with a plan but her mind was blank. All she could focus on was helping her friend. *He has to live,* she thought. *Please let him live.*

***

Key hovered in darkness, trying to find his way back to reality. Sometimes he could hear Aurora humming. Other times he could hear Sam and Nanny's voices, talking or arguing about his father. *His father.* He didn't want to think about his father. When he thought about Aurora, he felt peace. He pictured her face in his mind, and slowly the darkness melted into light.

"Wake up" a stern but familiar voice said, shaking him slightly. "*Kanaka ʻopio,* I need to speak to you."

Key opened his eyes to a room filled with bright white light, and a woman was standing beside him. She smiled and took his hand, squeezing it lightly.

"Who are you?" he asked.

She remained silent, still smiling at him. There were pink flowers entwined in her wavy brown hair, and there was something familiar about her face.

"Go see the whales," she said. "Take Rory to see the whales again."

Key studied her features- her deep brown eyes, soft like velvet- the color of her skin, tan from the sun. Her image faded and suddenly he was standing in the New Cemetery, watching the whales from a distance. A plume of water formed rainbows above their heads and their melancholy songs filled the air. *"Go see the whales, kanaka'opio."*

Key heard the whales one last time and his eyes opened wide. Aurora was asleep in a chair beside his bed.

***

"*Aurora*!" a strong voice said.

Aurora jolted from her sleep and looked around, only to find that she was no longer in the Kind Doctor's cottage. She was in the New Cemetery, but somehow it looked different. The grass was bright green, the sky turquoise blue. In the distance, she could hear the whales singing, and their songs sounded happy.

"Aurora," the same voice said from behind her. Aurora turned to see a woman standing near the cliff, dressed in white. She had brown hair and dark eyes - she looked familiar somehow but Aurora couldn't place it. The woman was barefoot and a shiny blue stone glistened from her necklace. She smiled warmly at Aurora and pointed towards the sea, in the direction of the whales.

"It's there," the woman said.

"What's there?" Aurora asked, looking towards the sea. A whale flipped its tail in the water, but beyond that, she saw nothing.

"I'm glad he found you," the woman said. "We are not so different, you and I. Take care of him for me."

She reached out to touch Aurora's hand. "*Find it, Aurora*," she said urgently.

Her name echoed several times in the air as the woman's image disappeared before her eyes. "Aurora...*Aurora...Rory...*"

Aurora blinked her eyes and lifted her head. She had fallen asleep next to Key's bed.

"Rory?" Key said softly.

"Key?" she exclaimed in surprise. The woman's voice still lingered in her mind, intertwined with Key's. She leaned forward and hugged him with relief.

"Are you okay? Are you in pain?"

"I'm fine," he said. "I feel a lot better. How are you?"

"*Me?*" she laughed through happy tears. "I'm great now that you're awake. I thought you were giving up on me. I thought you were going to leave me here."

"I wouldn't do that," Key said, speaking slowly.

Aurora touched his forehead where Samuel had stitched a deep laceration. Dried blood was still caked in his hair.

"Rory," he said again.

Aurora's eyes widened. "Why do you keep calling me that?"

"I don't know," Key replied. "I heard that name in my mind."

"From who?"

Key closed his eyes and tried to remember. "I don't know."

"That was my nickname," Aurora said.

"She called you that," Key added. "She said Rory."

"Who?"

"The lady. She said I should take Rory to see the whales again."

"What are you talking about?" Aurora asked in disbelief. "What lady?"

"Kanakaʻopio."

Aurora took a step back from Key's bedside. "What did you say?"

"*Kanakaʻopio*," Key repeated. "What does that mean?"

"You tell me."

"I don't know what it means."

Aurora's knees felt weak. She pulled a chair to Key's bedside and collapsed in disbelief. Her hands were shaking. "My mother called me Rory."

Key looked at Aurora in shock. "She looked like you!" he exclaimed. "The woman I saw looked like you! She had flowers in her hair. She said *Kanaka 'opio*. What does that mean?"

Aurora couldn't believe what she was hearing. "Young man," she finally said. "*Kanaka 'opio* means young man on The Green Islands. Key...did you...*see*...my mother?"

Key shook his head. "I don't...I don't know?"

Aurora was speechless. For a moment she sat in silence, then suddenly, she remembered. "I...I think I saw your mother, too."

"What?"

"She was in the New Cemetery. She pointed to the whales. She said we could find it there."

"Find what?"

"I don't know. She just pointed but I didn't see anything, just the whales."

"The whales were in my dream, too."

"What else did the woman- my mother- say in your dream?" Aurora couldn't believe her own words.

"She was just...there...and then she wasn't...and then the whales were making a rainbow and she said 'take Rory to see the whales.' That's all I remember."

"I don't know what that means."

"What else did the woman say in *your* dream? How do you know it was my mother?"

"She looked like you," Aurora said. "She said she was glad you found me and that we weren't so different. She was dressed all in white and she had a shiny necklace on. It was a stone."

Key's eyes widened. "Was it blue?"

"Yes!" Aurora gasped.

"That was my mother's favorite necklace. She never took it off. She was wearing it the night...the night she died."

"How is this possible?" Aurora gasped. "You dreamt of my mother and I dreamt of yours?"

Aurora was relieved that Key was awake and in good spirits, but suddenly she felt angry. All of this time without her parents, without her mother. There were no signs, no apparitions, no symbolic dreams. As much as she hoped and prayed, they never visited her. In the beginning, her dreams were just nightmares of the wreck; now they were dark and colorless. She pleaded for signs from above, but nothing ever came. No one came.

"Why would she visit you and not me? Why would I see *your* mother and not my own?"

"I don't know," Key replied, trying to sit up. Aurora placed some pillows behind him and helped him get comfortable. Some of his ribs were broken and wrapped tightly in bandages. He winced when he tried to move. "I don't understand any of this."

"I should call Samuel," Aurora said, standing up. Maybe they were both going crazy. Maybe they were finally losing their minds after everything they had been through. Key grabbed her hand.

"I don't know what I saw or if it was a dream, but it felt real," he said.

"So did my dream," Aurora admitted. "I can't explain it, but I think it was important. I could *feel* how important it was."

"Well one thing I do know for sure- my father did this to me."

"I know," Aurora nodded. "I found you on the shore. I was worried when you didn't come back from fishing so I went looking for you."

"Someone saw us by the bluffs. That night," Key took a breath between words. It was difficult to talk. "someone saw us and they told him. They told Lorn."

Aurora hung her head, somehow feeling to blame. Their magical moment together had been marked and tainted. "I thought you were dead. When I saw you lying on the shore, I thought he killed you."

"I'm sorry," Key said.

"No!" Aurora snapped. "Don't say that! Don't be sorry anymore! It's not your fault, it's *his* fault! And I get it now, Key, I do. The more time I spend here, the more I feel like one of you. I want to give up. I want to keep quiet and mind my business. I'm afraid for my life, I'm afraid for *your* life. Maybe that's why our mothers came to us in dreams. Even if it wasn't real, it's another sign that we have to get off this island before it kills us both."

It seemed like a hundred years ago when they sat in the New Cemetery, sketching ideas in Key's notebook and making plans to escape. Now everything seemed impossible, their ideas erased. Key didn't even have the strength to lift his head, let alone build a boat.

"I will take you to see the whales again," Key said. "Like your mother told me, and you can show me where my mother was pointing."

Aurora nodded. "I would like that, but what good will it do." Her last words fell flat. It was not a question.

"Maybe it really was a sign," Key said. "Maybe there's something we're missing."

Aurora sighed, not sure what to make of their cryptic dreams. "You need to heal," she said. "That's the plan. Get better. Then maybe we'll go see the whales and figure it out from there."

In the back of her mind, Aurora wanted to kill Lorn. That was the plan she was concocting on her own. He was five times her size but her mind was spinning- could she poison him? Hit him over the head? Push him off a cliff? Smother him while he slept? As much as she despised this man, the thought of taking his life was terrifying. Even if doing so allowed them to escape, she could not live free and happy at the expense of another, no matter how disgusting he was. Her parents would not have wanted it that way. And so she nodded and smiled at Key, promising their plans would continue, promising to watch the whales. But truthfully she felt hopeless and trapped.

CHAPTER 13

In the weeks it took Key to heal, Aurora visited the New Cemetery every day. She used London's spy glass to watch the whales and waited patiently for a sign- a flash, a glimmer of hope- *anything* from the heavens above. But nothing ever came. And she began to wonder if their visions were just dreams or strange coincidences that meant nothing at all. And one day when Key was well enough to join her there, he admitted the same thing.

"Our minds can play funny tricks on us sometimes," he said sadly as he sketched the whales in his notebook. "Maybe they were just realistic dreams."

"But then how did you know she called me Rory? How did we *both* dream about our moms?"

"I don't know, maybe when you were sitting by my bed, our brainwaves crossed."

"Oh, come on, that seems like a stretch."

"And visions from the other side don't?"

Aurora sighed. The whale's songs echoed in the sky and she closed her eyes. She felt like a fool for believing in something so outlandish. Another part of her felt angry at her parents for not reaching out to her, angry at her mother for reaching out to Key.

Regardless, they stayed at the New Cemetery till the sky grew dark. The moon and stars were covered by clouds and they could no longer see the whales. Key put an arm around Aurora, sensing her hopelessness. They both felt defeated, sensing their brief messages from the heavens were really just cruel tricks.

"We'll think of something," Key said reassuringly, but in his heart he had no idea what to do next.

Aurora bowed her head, but when she looked up, something unusual caught her eye.

"What is that?"

Key glanced in the direction she was looking but saw nothing, only darkness.

"*There!*" she said again, pointing. "By the rocks! Something's floating!"

At first Key thought something was floating in the water, and he wondered how Aurora could see that in the dark. But then he caught sight of it, too, and it wasn't in the water at all. There was a small dim light, bobbing in the air near the rocks.

"Give me the spyglass!" Aurora said, pulling it from Key's pocket before he could respond.

She struggled to focus the small device in the darkness, scanning left and right till she found the mysterious light source.

"Something's shining," Aurora said. "I can't make out what it is but it's flickering."

"We need to get down there," Key said, but Aurora was already a step ahead of him, heading down the hill and motioning for him to follow.

***

The darkness didn't slow them down but Key's condition did. Although he was mostly healed, he had lost his agility and felt winded climbing the rocks. But they pressed on, staying close to the water and the perimeter of the island so no one would see them. They followed the sound of the whales, knowing they were getting closer as the songs grew louder.

"I think it was here," Aurora said, looking over her shoulder, back up the hill towards the direction of the

New Cemetery. "This looks like the spot but I don't see anything."

They both scanned the darkness for shining lights or flashing like they had seen through the spyglass, but nothing appeared.

"Do you think it was an illusion?" Key asked.

Aurora shook her head. "No, there is something here and there is something our mothers wanted us to see. I know it now. I can *feel* it."

She walked up and down the shoreline and her boots crunched across the wet stones. *"Pffffssssshhhh!"* the whales spouted and the sound hissed through the air. When Aurora turned her head to watch them, a sudden glimmer appeared in her peripheral vision.

"There!" she cried, running towards the light.

Key struggled to keep up with her as she ran across the gravely shore. He could see the glimmery light now, too, and his heart beat faster in his chest.

A trick of the eye, an illusion, two giant boulders situated *just so* on Graystone Island wound up hiding a small alcove, not far from the original trade dock location. When Aurora and Key rounded the corner, they saw this alcove, and the source of the mysterious light near a small cave.

Lodged between the rocks above the narrow cave was a shiny blue stone. Key recognized it immediately and so did

Aurora, since it was the same stone that once hung from the neck of Mariana Terek. A tarnished silver chain was still attached to it, weathered and knotted but intact. It appeared to have been tangled in the rocks for many years, since debris and algae had grown around it. It was wet and still shiny, so it sparkled when the bright moonlight hit it.

"Is *this* what they wanted us to find?" Aurora said, trying to mask her disappointment.

Key jumped down from the rocks into the shallow water near the cave. The water sloshed around his ankles but he reached up and tugged at the necklace, hoping to release it.

"It's amazing that we saw it from so far away."

Key said nothing and tugged at the necklace again. When it didn't come free he pulled with both hands, anger and sadness fueling him.

"Be careful!" Aurora warned.

"She was wearing this when she died," Key said. "She never took it off."

He pulled hard one last time and the necklace gave way, launching him backwards into the water. Aurora gasped and leaped over to help him, and as she did so, both of them caught sight of something bobbing up and down inside the cave. There, between the narrow walls of the rocks, was a boat.

They both stood in the ankle deep water, not believing what they were seeing. Key gripped the blue stone tightly in his fist, its chain dangling above his knee. They stood in silence, staring in disbelief at the tattered brown boat until Aurora finally let out a gasp. Her hands shook as she sloshed forward in the water to touch its wooden sides.

"I don't believe it," she said.

Key got as close to the boat as he could in the shallow cave, anxious to see what condition it was in. The boat bobbed softly in the wake of the Baric waters, perfectly shielded from high waves by the arched rock walls. The alcove cliffs had kept the boat hidden through the years, tucked away from wind and rain.

"High tide must cover this alcove," Key realized. "I'm thinking this whole area can only be accessed at certain times of the year during low tide."

"When the whales are here," Aurora added.

"Yes," Key agreed. He couldn't see much of the boat in the darkness, so he was running his hands along the sides of it, trying to assess its condition.

"It's a sailing dinghy," Aurora said. "And it's still floating, that's a good sign."

"Yes," Key agreed. "But I think we have to see it in the daylight to be sure."

Aurora wanted to pull the boat out and immediately sail away but she knew that wasn't wise. They needed to make sure the boat was stable, they needed supplies. So they agreed to return to the alcove the next afternoon, when Key had completed his fishing duties.

***

What Key and Aurora eventually discovered was that the little dinghy was only accessible during low tide, which typically happened at night. They tried visiting the alcove at various times throughout the day, including morning, but it was always flooded over. The water was too high, too rough, and too dangerous to traverse. So Aurora and Key met in the darkness to assess the boat's condition, and told no one of what they had found. They brought a change of clothing, blankets, and a lantern to guide them.

Accessing the dinghy was no easy task, since the water in the alcove was about 5 feet deep and cold as ice. The cave where the boat was hidden was narrow with a low ceiling- too dark to see anything with the naked eye. They brought a lantern and extra layers of clothing, deciding that Aurora should be the one to squeeze into the cave to inspect the boat. They were too scared to pull the dinghy from its hiding space just yet. The thought of exposing something so precious to the harshness of Graystone Island was too frightening. They did not want to risk the only chance they had for escape.

"There's a bag here," Aurora said, holding a dim lantern as she squeezed into the small cave and examined the boat's interior.

"Can you reach it?"

Aurora stretched her arm into the dinghy and pulled out a burlap bag. It was damp from the sea air but otherwise intact. She handed it to Key and held the lantern closer to the boat's deck. From her brief inspection she could see no holes or leaks. There was a canvas sail rolled up on the floor of the boat but it was too heavy for her to lift with one hand. She passed Key the lantern and leaned awkwardly over the side of the boat, trying not to hit her head on the rocks above. She reached blindly into the dinghy, felt for the sail and grabbed it with both hands, hoisting it over the edge to Key. Her teeth chattered and her legs ached from the harsh water temperature, so she quickly made her way back to dry land with Key to inspect what they had found.

"I couldn't see any holes," she said, shaking from the cold. "I didn't see any leaks, nothing noticeable anyway."

Key wrapped her in a thick blanket as she sat down on the pebbly shore. Her hands shook as she changed her wet shoes and socks.

"The boat is so small, Key," Aurora said. "We can't go far."

"We can go far enough," Key replied, inspecting the rolled up sail with his lantern.

"The Blue Coast. We could make it there with the right conditions," she stated.

Key and Aurora locked eyes in the darkness as soon as she said the words. The Blue Coast had been his mother's dream and London's home. He immediately grabbed the canvas bag they had found on the boat and dumped its contents onto the dark, pebbly shore. They had planned to wait and bring the bag back to the cottage, but Key needed to see what was inside.

A handful of items tumbled onto the rocks - some canned food from Graystone Market, several empty water flasks, bandages, some matches. They stared at the items in the darkness. Key shook the bag one more time and a small blank sketchbook fell out, followed by a tattered box of colored pencils. Key recognized them instantly and gasped.

"Ohhh," Aurora's mouth fell open in shock.

Key picked up the pencils and rolled them around in his hand. "I can't believe it."

"This was your mother's boat, wasn't it?" Aurora said. "*She* hid this boat!"

"I think she did," Key replied hesitantly.. "I...I thought she was waiting for London that night...the night my father darkened the lighthouse."

"She needed the light for herself," Aurora said. "For both of you."

"All this time I thought she was waiting for London...but *she* had the boat."

"Key," Aurora said softly. "Is it possible London is still alive?"

Key said nothing.

"Did you actually see his boat that night? Did you hear a wreck?"

"My mother was screaming," Key replied. "I assumed she had been waiting for him. She told me he was going to help us."

"Maybe he was the one who helped her *get* the boat. Maybe he helped her hide it?"

"I don't...I don't know," Key was filled with a mixture of anger and sadness. He had misunderstood everything for so many years. He wished his mother had told him. *Why hadn't she told him?* Maybe he could have helped, maybe he could have made it to the boat that night. Remorse flooded over him. There was so much more he could have done.

"Don't do this to yourself," Aurora said, reading his thoughts. "She had her reasons. She wanted to protect you."

"She failed."

"No she didn't! You're still here, Key. You're *alive!*" Aurora snatched up the items and began shoving them back in the canvas bag. "If you're going to be mad at someone, be mad at Lorn. We're a step ahead of him now and we found what your mother hid all those years ago. I can't explain it but I think she fought her way back from the dead just to show you, Key."

As crazy as it seemed, Key knew in his heart this was true. Both of their mothers had guided them here. And the boat was exactly where they needed it to be, by the deepest waters of the island. He knew it was safe to launch where the whales could swim.

"Two days," Key said firmly. "Let's go two days from now. That's plenty of time to prepare and tie up loose ends. We can make it to the Blue Coast, I know we can."

"Then what?"

Key stood up, holding the sketchbook tightly. His mother's hope was in his hands now.

"I don't know," he said. "But we'll figure it out together."

***

There wasn't much for Aurora to pack because she had nothing. She would sail from Graystone with the clothes on her back and provisions for the journey, yet somehow she felt like she was leaving everything behind. The island took her family from her, and leaving it would mean letting go, like releasing the string of a balloon. She was excited to leave, yet that invisible string would always tug at her heart.

Key had inspected the sail and there was only one weathered spot that Aurora was able to patch. They had a canvas bag of provisions- canned goods, water, some first aid supplies and matches. Aurora found a compass in Samuel's drawer and she hoped he wouldn't miss it because they needed it desperately. Key had no idea how to find his way to the Blue Coast but Aurora did. She promised that with a compass and the stars she could find her way across the whole world. Their plan was in motion, the boat was packed and ready. Tomorrow, at midnight, they would sail.

CHAPTER 14

"Samuel," Aurora said in a soft voice. "Did you know that Key uses the seabirds to help him find fish in the morning?"

Samuel glanced at Aurora from behind his tiny bifocals. She was sitting by the fire in Nanny's rocking chair, darning a sock. She rocked slowly back and forth, and the chair creaked loudly against the floor.

"No, my dear, I didn't know that." Samuel replied, closing the book he was reading.

"Yes," Aurora continued. "He waits to see where the seagulls dive, and that's where he throws the nets."

Samuel nodded, ready to resume his reading before Aurora spoke again.

"He baits hooks, too, and sets them out all at the same time," Aurora explained. "And if there are no big fish close to shore, he waits for the little ones to attract them."

Aurora looked over at Samuel, making sure that he had heard her. He smiled at her kindly, not understanding her motive. Aurora cared deeply for the Alcids. Without them she most certainly would have perished on Graystone Island. She wanted to make sure they were taken care of. *Remember what I have told you,* Aurora thought, *So that when we are gone, you will be able to survive.*

Aurora felt guilty about leaving the Alcids behind, especially after all they had done for her. But there was no room in the tiny dinghy, and not enough provisions for four travelers. She also knew that the Alcids considered Graystone their home. Their ancestors had lived on the island for centuries, and their loyalty remained, no matter what conditions they endured.

"Such a sweet child," Samuel said as he stood up from the sofa. "helping Key the way you do, and trying to teach an old man like me the ways of the sea."

Aurora had an immediate urge to tell Samuel their plan. But it was imperative that she keep the journey a secret, even from the Alcids. She did not want to endanger them if Lorn ever found out- nor did she want them objecting to the journey and trying to convince them to stay.

"Key gets paid fifty coins for his catches at the market," Aurora added. "And sometimes Johnson Laridae will give him double if he brings the freshest fish straight to the tavern."

"So good for Key," Samuel nodded. "Such a smart boy."

Aurora took one last glance at the Kind Doctor in his cozy living room. Her heart filled with gratitude and sadness as she stood and hugged him. He chuckled in surprise and patted her arm.

"Goodnight, Samuel," she said. "Sleep well."

***

Key took the canned sardines from Nanny and placed them on the highest pantry shelf for her.

"One more," she said, handing him a second can. "My tall helper."

Guilt washed over Key but he did his best to stifle it. "You know you have a stepstool, Nanny," Key replied. "You don't need me."

She laughed and shook her head. "It's easier if you do it."

Key assessed the pantry. He could see that Sam and Nanny were well-stocked, but still he worried about them managing after he was gone. He tried to remind himself that they had always managed, even long before he arrived. They would have even more food in storage with two less mouths to feed.

"Nanny, you know I'm grateful for you, right?"

"And I'm grateful for you, Key," she responded. "You're a good boy. *No-*" she paused, correcting herself. "*Man.* You are a good *man*, Key."

Key smiled and hugged her tightly. For the first time, he *did* feel like a man. He had a purpose and a love that he wanted to protect for the rest of his life. He felt proud and responsible for their journey ahead. But he was also terrified. He wasn't sure if the boat was seaworthy or exactly how long the journey would be. He was scared of the danger around Graystone and the darkness of the sea, but the thought of staying on the island was even more terrifying than leaving.

Aurora's arrival, their mothers' mysterious messages and the discovery of the boat seemed written in the stars. Everything had aligned for them to take this journey, and they were ready.

CHAPTER 15

The next morning, Key completed his fishing duties as usual. Even though he avoided crossing paths with Lorn, he knew his father kept tabs on him. If he failed to show up with the fishing supply, Lorn would be notified. Key's plan was business as usual, tie up loose ends, double-check their supplies, and head out at midnight. It was a good, tight plan. But somewhere in between, something went terribly wrong.

Key returned to The Kind Doctor's cottage at noon to have lunch with Aurora, but before he could even reach the door, an explosive sound filled the air. He dropped all of his fishing gear in shock and immediately covered his head. Aurora came running from the cottage, her face filled with fear.

"What was that noise?" she screamed. "Are those gun-shots?"

BANG! BANG! The sounds continued above the distant crashing waves. "Where is it coming from?"

"Near the shore, I think," Key said. "Where are Sam and Nanny?"

"They're on house call," Aurora replied. "What's going on?"

Cries of screaming sea birds filled the air, followed by an odd, muffled, "*arrr-ARRR, arrr-ARRR!*"

Panic seized Key's heart when he recognized the puffin's alert call. They would only make that sound if their lives were in danger. "The puffins!" he cried. "Come on!"

Key ran towards the puffin roost, holding Aurora's hand.

"What's happening?" she cried above the noise of the birds.

The explosive sound had stopped but the birds were clearly still agitated. As Aurora and Key neared the roost, they could see corpses of puffins littering the rocks, leaking dark red blood into the sea. Their limp bodies were strewn along the shore in a gory trail.

Key had grown up around these puffins. He considered them friends; comical little birds that helped him fish and entertained him with natural antics when he was lonely.

The villagers believed it was a bad omen to harm puffins. There was no profit in their meat, no purpose to slaughtering them.

Aurora and Key stopped in their tracks when they reached the shore. Lorn was standing among bodies of bloody puffins, holding a gun in one hand and a liquor bottle in the other. He didn't notice Key at first, but was yelling, *"BOY!* Where are you, *boy?"*

Lorn staggered along the rocks, kicking at the lifeless bodies. Key was so outraged that he screamed, ***"FATHER!"*** without considering the consequences. He lunged at Lorn, slamming into him from behind and knocking him to the ground. The liquor bottle shattered against the rocks.

Lorn cursed in anger and rolled over, punching Key in the face and head. Aurora screamed and started beating him with her fists, but it was like punching a brick wall. Unfazed, he pushed her away and she fell backwards, tumbling into the broken glass. Pain seared her arm as some of the shards cut right through her sweater. Blood soaked through her sleeve as she pulled a small shard of glass from her elbow.

Key screamed her name, kicking Lorn in the stomach. When he doubled over, gasping for air, Key kicked him again and again until he stopped moving. Then he kicked the gun away from Lorn and ran to Aurora.

"What is he doing here?" Aurora cried. There was glass in her hair and a gash across her cheek. *"Why is he doing this?"*

"Are you okay?" Key asked, pulling the glass from her hair. "Hurry, we need to get out of here. He's insane, he'll kill us both-"

In seconds, Lorn was on his feet again, taking Key by surprise. Lorn swung a powerful fist at Key's head, temporarily dazing him. Key struggled to remain conscious, but the world was already spinning. He reached out for Aurora, wanting to tell her to run, run to the boat and don't look back. But Lorn intercepted with a final, debilitating blow. Key fell limp across the rocks. Lorn had somehow located his gun and now cocked the blood-splattered revolver at Key's head.

"*NO!*" Aurora screamed in shock.

But it was too late. Aurora lunged for the gun just as Lorn pulled the trigger. She fell to the ground, expecting the final shot to deafen her ears, but there was only a hollow click.

The gun was empty.

Lorn swore beneath his breath and Aurora leaped at him, punching him repeatedly, scratching at his face and cursing him incoherently. But she was like a rag doll in comparison and he hurled her through the air towards the cliff side. Her body slammed into the rocks and crumbled to the ground where she lay motionless. Lorn reached down and grabbed Key's collar.

"You've disobeyed me for the last time," he muttered, and began dragging Key back to the Darkhouse.

CHAPTER 16

There was a ringing in Aurora's ears, followed by a rushing sound that brought her back to reality. She opened her eyes to gray-white sky and birds - birds *everywhere*- flying, swooping, and filling the air with noise. Her entire body ached and blood seeped into her eye, blurring her vision. She sat up, clutching her side and scanning the shoreline. Limp puffin bodies littered the rocks, and the tide was pulling some of them out to sea. Aurora scanned the shoreline for Key and Lorn but they were nowhere to be found. While she sat on the ground struggling to focus, she noticed marks in the dirt, leading away from the shore. It looked like something- someone- had been dragged. *Key.* Her stomach churned. The thought of making it across the island to the Darkhouse seemed impossible, but she needed to find Key. There was a chance he was still alive and she wasn't leaving Graystone Island without him.

***

The islanders were outraged when they saw Lorn dragging Key's lifeless body through the village. But they were not outraged by Lorn's actions. They were angry at Key.

"Puffin killer!" they called, spitting at Key's feet. "Punish him!"

Key Terek brought bad omens to Graystone Island. The abandonment of his mother, the Green girl, now puffin killing. Lorn made certain that the villagers understood this as he passed by. He made no effort to hide Key's condition. Instead, he flaunted what he had done to his son and announced his intentions.

"Justice will be served," he promised them. "I will take care of Key myself."

***

Aurora was losing hope as she approached the Darkhouse. It stood ominous and tall ahead of her and she struggled to reach it, chest aching and head pounding. The wind blew her hair into her eyes and howled in her ears, but she pressed on, determined.

And then she saw them.

Gathered around the Darkhouse cottage were several hunched figures, dressed in gray. Their walking sticks were adorned with tiny bells that jingled in the wind, but Aurora couldn't hear them from a distance. The Elders were gathered around the Darkhouse cottage door, waiting.

She stopped in her tracks and knew a split second decision had to be made. The Elders were strangers to her and she trusted no one, but they seemed to be the only form of law on Graystone. So she took a chance and shouted loudly, *"HELP!"*

All of their heads turned as she ran towards them.

***

Key awoke on a cold, hard floor and for a moment he wasn't sure where he was. But then he heard the muffled sound of waves crashing below and saw the arched wooden ceiling above him. The walls were glass instead of stone, and through them he could see an empty gray-white sky. He was in the Darkhouse lantern room, the very tip of the tower. He had not been in this room for many years, but the musty odor, the faraway sound of crashing waves, and the shattered lantern were all the same. How and why Key ended up here was a mystery, but he knew he had to get out. He could sense danger here, like the feeling of reaching a dead end with nowhere to turn. As he struggled to get to his feet, the first word that floated into his mind was *AGAIN.*

How had this happened again?

How many times was Lorn going to beat him senseless? And more importantly, how much longer until Lorn killed him? He was certain that his time on Graystone was fleeting. An end was near- although he wasn't exactly sure what kind. He just knew that he had to get out. *Get out, get out, get out,* his brain told him. He rolled to his left to find the scuttle hole; it wasn't a door exactly, just a hatch in the floor. It was the only way into the lantern room from below. Lorn must have carried him all the way up the spiral stone staircase of the Darkhouse to get here, but Key didn't have time to wonder why. He tugged on the hatch door but it wouldn't budge. Sliding to his knees, he took hold of the metal latch and pulled as hard as he could. The door would not move, and Key knew that Lorn must have sealed him in somehow, since the scuttle hatch had no lock. He kicked at it and pounded it with his fists but it was no use. Key was trapped.

***

"Please help!" Aurora cried. The words spilled from her mouth without thought. "Lorn beat Key and dragged him here! We must help him!"

At that moment, the cottage door whipped open and Aurora flinched, stumbling backwards as Lorn's hulking figure stepped outside. He scowled at her but then turned away and bowed his head.

"My Elders," he said. "I am humbled by your presence."

"Lorn," one of the Elders said, reaching out to touch his shoulder. Lorn had to bend slightly to allow the old man to reach. "It's been many years."

Lorn touched the Elder's shoulder in return.

"We heard about the incident on the shore," a female Elder said in a stern voice.

Aurora waited silently, holding her breath.

Lorn sighed dramatically. "My apologies, dear Elders."

"We are disappointed," another added. "We had to come. You know this is a serious matter."

"Yes," Lorn responded. " I am sorry, my Elders, for this shame."

Aurora opened her mouth to speak but another Elder quickly called out, "It is not your fault, Lorn."

Aurora spun her head in shock to stare at the woman who had spoken.

"I thought I raised him better," Lorn sighed. "I warned him you would come. I have failed you."

"What is going on here?" Aurora snapped.

"*Green* girl!" one of The Elders hissed.

"You know who I am?"

"Of course," an Elder male replied. "We know all about you, foreigner."

"My name is Aurora."

"We know who you are."

"Your mouth is too quick, *Green* girl," an Elder said. "You have no business here!"

"I have business here! Key is injured!" Aurora shouted. "Lorn beat him unconscious. We need to find Key, quickly!"

"*Key*," an Elder stressed, "committed a serious crime. Puffin killing is not taken lightly here."

"Key needs to be punished," another Elder added.

"You are mad!" she snapped. "It was LORN who killed the puffins! He beat us both when we tried to stop him!"

"I have no reason to kill puffins," Lorn laughed. "You are the one who is mad."

"Be gone, Green girl, so we can continue our business."

"What business? Your business should be finding Key! He will tell you himself!"

"We *are* here for Key!" an Elder snapped back. "We know all."

"Do you? Do you know that Lorn killed Mariana Terek?"

The Elders gasped collectively.

"Shut your mouth, girl! That's a lie!" Lorn growled.

"How dare you make such accusations!"

"Mariana Terek abandoned her family. She left her husband and son for a foreign trader almost a decade ago," a female Elder said.

"That's what Lorn told you but it's not true. *HE KILLED HER!* I swear to you, he's a *murderer!*"

"The only murderer here is Key," one of the Elders chimed in. "And you, foreign girl, need to mind your business."

Aurora desperately searched their faces for any sign of sympathy or support, but their expressions were cold. Their eyes were like Lorn's. Aurora realized from their faces that these were *Lorn's* Elders. They were *all* Lorn's Elders.

"Where are Mariana's Elders?"

"Why do you ask this? You have no authority here!"

"If Key is to be punished then I think *all* of his Elders should be present," Aurora said. "I want to know what Mariana's Elders think of this, and what *they* think of her disappearance!"

"Do not raise your voice to us, child," a female Elder warned.

"Then bring forth her Elders," Aurora urged. "and let them judge."

"I am sorry for this disrespect, my Elders-" Lorn interrupted.

"Why does she keep making demands?"

"She is brazen," Lorn said with a sneer.

"You are tiring us, girl."

"If I tire you then bring them forth," Aurora repeated.

"Why does she make foolish requests?"

Aurora frowned. "Why is that a foolish request?"

"Because *Mariana has no Elders here!*" one man finally snapped. "Now mind your business and move on!"

"What do you mean?" she asked, "No Elders *here*? What does that mean?"

"What do you think it means, girl? Go away!"

One of the Elders pointed a cane and prodded her shoulder. "You need to leave now, foreigner. We know the trouble your kind brings."

"Where are Mariana's Elders?" Aurora questioned again. "I demand to see them!"

The Elders let out another collective gasp and Lorn watched them warily, staying silent.

"You demand?"

"The nerve!"

"You have no right to demand!"

"Why won't you bring them here?" Aurora questioned, raising her voice. "What happened to them? *Where are they?*"

"Why would she have Elders here?" the head Elder finally snapped.

"Well, why wouldn't she?" Aurora cried. "All Elders reside on this island."

"True islanders have Elders here, not foreigners!"

Silence followed and it took Aurora a moment to respond. "Mariana Terek was not born on Graystone Island?"

"Of course not!" an Elder snapped.

"Enough!" Lorn shouted. "Get out of here, girl! You poison our people!" He shoved Aurora in the chest but this time she did not fall. The puzzle pieces clicked together as she recalled Mariana's words in her head.

We are not so different, you and I.

"Mariana was from the Green Islands, wasn't she?"

Lorn stared straight ahead, avoiding her eyes.

Aurora remembered what Key had told her, that his mother married Lorn because he helped her, because she needed him.

"Is Key even your son?" Aurora questioned. "Where is the truth here, Lorn?"

"ENOUGH!" Lorn lunged at Aurora but the Elders held up their canes to stop him. Aurora pushed past Lorn and ran inside the cottage.

"Key!" she screamed.

A commotion followed behind her but she ran from room to room of the small cottage, searching for Key and calling his name.

CHAPTER 17

Attempting to open the lantern room scuttle hatch was futile. Whatever Lorn secured the door with was very heavy and no matter how hard Key tried, the hatch remained sealed. He assessed the room, trying not to lose hope. Just as he remembered, the Darkhouse lantern was cracked and broken. Lorn had shattered it years ago with a sledgehammer, ensuring that the Baric waters would remain dark forever. There was only one glass door in the tower and it opened outwards, towards the sea. A narrow, railed ledge ran along the tower, barely wide enough for one person to walk. The hatch door at his feet was blocked. The room was empty except for a bundle of thick rope on the floor and some old liquor bottles. But something else in the room caught Key's eye. Lorn had certainly smashed the Darkhouse lantern to pieces, but he left the original source of its light.

He left the whale oil.

At one time, whale oil had been used to light the enormous Darkhouse lantern. They had collected this precious whale oil from years of visiting trade ships. The supply still remained hidden in the lantern room so Lorn could ration it out to villagers at his discretion.

Key had always known the whale oil was there, so perhaps the plan brewing in his mind had been lingering silently for years, waiting for the right moment to come forward.

Key's fishing bag was still draped across his shoulder from the morning duties. His beloved sketchbook was tucked inside, along with some simple tools - a rag, a ball of twine, extra fishing line, a dull switchblade, and a pack of matches. Key never used the matches much and often left them behind for fear of getting them wet. But this morning had been colder than usual, and he anticipated building a fire on the shoreline.

Key didn't stop to wonder why he was executing this dormant plan, or if it was even the right thing to do. He just removed the rag from his pouch and tossed it on the floor. He poured some whale oil over the rag, across the floor, along the railing, wherever it would reach. Its pungent, fishy odor filled the room and Key choked at the stench. He spilled as much of the oil as he could, careful not to get any on himself. Then he opened the glass door, pushing firmly against the wind, and stepped outside. The wind howled menacingly in Key's ears and stung his cheeks. Waves crashed against the rocks far, far below but he could barely hear them. When he looked out at the gray sky, a seagull flew by, cocking its head. Key clearly saw its yellow eye looking right back at him. He stepped back into the lantern room, questioning his own sanity. But that voice was still in his mind, nagging at him to *get out, get out, get out.* He pushed the door open again and peered over the railing. In one direction was the churning black sea and sharp rocks, but in the other direction was the top of the Darkhouse cottage. It was made of layers and layers of thatching, a style prominent throughout Graystone Island. Key tried to calculate the distance in his mind. Forty feet? Fifty? He stepped back into the lantern room and grabbed the rope. The sun was beginning to set and the room was already growing dark. Key moved quickly, knotting the rope over the sturdiest portion of the railing. His skill as a fisherman was vital- one wrong knot could cost him his life, so he triple checked, pulling and tugging the rope on the railing. Reaching into his tattered bag, he removed the pack of matches. He lit one, then the whole package, shielding it from the wind. The little wooden sticks glowed with yellow-orange embers as Key tossed the package onto the oily rag. With a quick *whoosh*, the rag ignited, and suddenly the whole floor was ablaze, snaking over the oil like a fiery reptile. The flames grew higher, swallowing the empty liquor bottles and creeping up the walls. Key squeezed out the glass door, shuffling along the railing. He grabbed the free end of the rope, loosely wrapping it around his waist and stepped over the edge. *What am I doing?* he thought. The flames were spreading faster now. Soon they would engulf the railing if he did not move quickly. So he gripped the rope and prepared to scale down the Darkhouse wall towards the cottage roof.

***

The cottage was empty and Aurora's time had run out. "What have you done with him?" she yelled at Lorn.

The Elders had lost all patience now and began swinging their sticks at her, shouting and cursing. One stick hit her in the middle of the back with a loud crack. Another barely missed her head; she heard *swoosh* as the stick whipped past her face.

"Get out, *get out!*" the Elders screamed, pushing her towards the door. Aurora stumbled backward through the front door, landing outside on the hard stone walkway. The last thing she saw was Lorn's face, smirking down at her as he slammed the door shut and latched it.

***

Get out, get out, the voice continued to repeat in Key's head. He tried very hard to concentrate on each step down but the wind was deafening and the wall of the Darkhouse was slippery. It was almost dark now and Key could barely see, but that was for the best since it masked the distance below him. The wind was so strong that it was actually pushing him as he scaled the wall, and he struggled to keep from dangling like a pendulum. The muscles in his arms burned under his own weight. He could see a stream of gray smoke beginning to pour from the lantern room above, but he couldn't hear or smell anything yet. He continued to inch slowly down the wall, holding his breath. His boot slipped on one of the bricks and he took a free fall for about five feet before catching himself again. In that brief moment of falling, he looked down at the dark ground below and caught a flash of movement. Key squinted his eyes in the twilight, realizing that a figure was standing below. He couldn't see much since the cottage was blocking his view, but somehow he managed to glimpse colors, or more precisely, a brightly colored dress hem blowing in the wind.

"*AURORA!*" he screamed.

Key had tried to remain calm during his descent but now he was beginning to panic. He didn't want her anywhere near the Darkhouse or Lorn.

"Run!" he screamed down to her. "Aurora! Run! Run, now! *Get to the boat!*"

It was obvious that she didn't hear him because she was walking towards the Darkhouse at a quick pace, not away from it. *No, no*, Key thought, *not that way*. "Not that way!" he screamed down to her, ignoring the task at hand. Suddenly he realized that he was out of rope.

***

Aurora scanned the area around the cottage, looking for any sign of Key. The sun was setting and it was already difficult to see in the shadowy crevices around the Darkhouse. *The Darkhouse.* Could Lorn have put Key in the Darkhouse? She did not want to go inside of that ominous tower but something told her that Key was inside, trapped and possibly dying. If Lorn had seen the Elders coming, he certainly would have wanted to hide Key to keep him from talking. Aurora took a deep breath and headed towards the door.

"AURORA!"

The sound of Key's voice somehow reached her on the wind, and she stopped in her tracks and looked around, seeing nothing.

"Key?" she called.

"AU..RA..." she could only make out pieces of what he was saying. He sounded very far away. "AU..DON'T...N OT..."

"Where are you?" she called again.

Key kicked his feet, trying to signal Aurora far below. He looked up and saw flames flickering out of the window.

"Get to the boat!" he yelled again. "The BOAT! Go! Go, now!"

He tugged desperately at the rope he was holding but there was nothing left. He was stuck, hanging on the side of the Darkhouse, and any minute the flames were going to be very obvious to the entire island.

Aurora couldn't find Key and she felt like she was walking in circles looking for him. He was not *in* the Darkhouse, that much she was sure of. His voice was coming to her in broken pieces, but she was able to make out some words, and they hit her like a flash: "Boat...go...now."

"Now?" she called back, unsure.

She didn't want to go to the boat without him, but in those few words she could hear desperation; he was pleading. Another split second decision was needed. She looked around one last time for him, trying not to panic. "Key! *Please!* Where are you?"

Key wished he could be a hero. He wished he could swoop down like a swashbuckling pirate and save the girl he loved. For he *did* love her and he could feel hope slipping away, along with his grip on the rope.

In his head he recalled the Kind Doctor's words after a distressing accident a few years back. One of the villagers had slipped from the cliffside and died. *"It's not the fall that kills you, Key, it's the landing."* Key glanced down at the thatched roof of the cottage. He wasn't sure exactly how far below it was, but it looked like a million miles. He unwrapped the remaining bit of rope from his waist and lowered himself as far down the wall of the Darkhouse as he could. Key closed his eyes, pressed both feet firmly against the tower, and propelled himself backward, letting go of the rope and stretching his arms wide as he did so.

For years Key had watched graceful seabirds soar through the sky above Graystone Island and longed to become one of them. He had followed their flapping wings with sad, young eyes, waiting for his turn to fly off into the fog. Now, like a wish haphazardly granted, he had found his own place in the sky.

Visions of black-backed terns and dusty shearwaters flashed through his mind, touching the water with their feet, cutting the sky with their wings. Down, down he flew, backwards as the wind screamed in his ears. It rushed past him with such sheer force that it felt like his clothes were being ripped from his body. *It's not the fall that kills you, Key, it's the landing.* Key opened his eyes at the last second and saw orange and yellow flames dancing atop the Darkhouse. They looked like arms reaching out for him.

It was over in seconds, yet the fall seemed like an eternity. He hit the thatched roof flat on his back, and debris shot up on all sides. The wind was completely knocked out of him and for a moment he couldn't breathe. He had no control over his body as physics propelled him sideways. He rolled in a heap down the sloped roof, gasping and tumbling towards the edge. His brain snapped into reality and he clawed his fingers into the surface in hopes of slowing his spiral, but it was no use. Key knew he was going to fall off the edge, and what a waste, he briefly thought, to survive one fall and not another. *It's not the fall that kills you, Key, it's the landing.*

***

Aurora ran just as Key jumped, and in the darkness she didn't see him above her, flying backwards just above her head. Hope was fading, but she ran, praying that Key was behind her or ahead of her, or somewhere near the boat since he told her to run. She was almost to the alcove when she noticed the glow; a faint, orange light, growing brighter and brighter. She turned just in time to see the top of the Darkhouse engulfed in flames, and she was hypnotized. *The sea was alive!* Everything glowed in shades of yellow and orange. Ocean waves danced with light and color, and wet rocks shimmered along the shore. Shadows everywhere, spinning, turning, splashing in and out of the water. But then her awe turned to fear. If the Darkhouse was on fire, where was Key?

***

Key hit the ground with a thud and the impact sent a shockwave through his entire body. He couldn't breathe and a sickening sound emerged from his throat as he tried to pump air back into his lungs. He had landed flat on his back, and as his eyes regained focus, he could see bright orange flames lighting the night sky. The Darkhouse was burning.

"What...have...you...*DONE!!!!*" Lorn's thunderous voice emerged from the cottage, disturbed by the commotion on the roof. The Elders followed in confusion, horrified by the flames and smoke.

The moment finally came when Key anticipated Lorn's next move. After he had fallen from the roof, a wave of bravery washed over him. He was tired of the pain and was no longer going to be caught off-guard. It was time to fight back. So the moment Lorn reached down to grab him, Key rolled to his left, grabbed a handful of gravel, and threw it in Lorn's face. Lorn howled in pain, clawing at his eyes. Key spotted a shovel leaning against the cottage and immediately grabbed it. He swung the shovel into the back of Lorn's knees, and Lorn collapsed to the ground, cursing. Key then raised the shovel over his head, using all of his anger and sadness as a driving force.

"No, Key!" a voice screamed.

Key froze, shovel in mid-air, and saw Aurora running towards him.

"Don't!!" she cried, "Don't do it, Key!"

Aurora had thought of killing Lorn herself, figuring it would be the only way to make him disappear. But now she knew that killing him would make him a part of their lives forever.

One swing. One swing and Key knew he could do it. Lorn would be done, never to hurt anyone again. One swing could avenge his mother and Aurora's parents. But then what? Key knew he couldn't run from horrible memories. Horrible memories stay.

Key yelled in frustration, throwing the shovel at Lorn instead of hitting him with it. The handle knocked Lorn on the forehead, and blood started to trickle down his face. One of the Elders shouted something incoherent, shuffling over to help Lorn. Lorn, still unable to see, lashed out violently, shoving the Elder away.

"Don't touch me!" he screamed.

The Elder flailed his arms and tumbled backward, knocking his head on a large boulder before hitting the ground with a thud. The remaining Elders gasped, but no one moved. The fallen Elder lay still, shadows dancing over his limp body from the flickering flames above. A large pool of blood began to form under his head, seeping into the gravel. The fallen Elder's walking stick had landed against the large boulder, and its bells jingled forebodingly in the wind. Key and Aurora watched, stunned, as the remaining Elders began sobbing and wailing.

Villagers were starting to arrive in a panic, having seen the flames. Many carried buckets of water and were dressed in sleepwear. Lorn finally rubbed the dirt from his eyes, exposing the scene of his anger. His mouth fell open in shock as he touched the Elder on the shoulder, shaking him slightly. The old man's hand flopped to the side, limp.

"What have you done?" one of the female Elders cried, echoing Lorn's own words. She knelt down and pulled the old man's body to her chest, sobbing.

"I didn't..." Lorn stuttered. "I didn't...realize."

Aurora reached out and slipped her hand into Key's. She stepped backwards, slowly urging him to follow. As the crowd of villagers and Elders gathered around Lorn, Key and Aurora slipped away into the darkness, but not before hearing the female Elder scream, "Lorn, you *killed* him! *You killed your own father!*"

CHAPTER 18

People were running through the village, trampling each other to get to the Darkhouse, their eyes wide with fear. Key and Aurora ran, too, but in the opposite direction, toward the alcove.

The smell of smoke permeated the air, and the sea was brightly lit with shades of orange and red. Aurora and Key could see every pebble at their feet as they ran to the boat, their last hope and salvation.

By the time they reached the alcove, Key knew the whole island was in a frenzy. They were too far away to hear or see what was happening now, but he could imagine their efforts to save the Darkhouse from destruction. He could still see Lorn's face in his mind- the look of shock and horror from his own violent outburst.

Key's shadow appeared at the alcove before they did, stretching across the shoreline in the Darkhouse's final, fiery glow. He raised his arms, amazed by the sight. Adrenaline coursed through Key's veins. Some of the wounds that had crusted over from Lorn's brutal beating were splitting open again, and Key could feel warm blood trickling down his arms and legs. Aurora helped to pull their boat from its hiding place, and it floated quietly through the shimmery water. An image of his mother and London flashed through Key's mind. He wished they could see this moment, this final departure. It was what his mother so desperately wanted. He wondered if she would be proud of him.

Aurora jumped into the boat and Key followed. They hoisted the small sail and it immediately popped open in the wind. The boat lurched forward and Key and Aurora held onto each other to steady themselves.

Key held his breath, waiting for a wave to knock them over or an unseen rock to crack their stern. He waited for someone to shout their names or a gust to push them into the reef. But the boat sailed swiftly on, cutting through the water with ease. When they were a good distance away from the island, Key looked back at the inferno and exhaled. Everything around them was quiet.

"You set it on fire," she said in admiration.

"It was the only way," Key replied, "to put an end to everything."

"What happens after it burns?"

Key shook his head. Perhaps the villagers would rebuild the Darkhouse, perhaps they would light it again. They had an opportunity to change things now, but he didn't know if they would. It didn't matter. The Darkhouse was not a part of him anymore.

"I'm proud of you," Aurora said. "Your mother would be proud of you."

Key nodded and bowed his head. Silence hung between them, waves lapping against the side of the boat.

"You once told me that your name is pointless," Aurora added. "But that isn't true at all. You were the key to everything. You were the key. You *are* the key...to my heart."

Key reached out and hugged her tightly, kissing her forehead. Aurora sobbed quietly as they embraced each other in the cold wind.

"I know it was hard not to use that shovel," she said. "But you are not like him."

"He killed his own father," Key said with disgust. "My grandfather."

Aurora inhaled sharply. "Maybe not."

"What do you mean?"

"The Elders told me Mariana was not an islander and that she had no relatives on Graystone," Aurora explained. "I believe your mother was from The Green Islands."

Key's eyes widened in shock.

"And I wondered if maybe..." Aurora paused, choosing her words carefully. "Maybe Lorn wasn't your real father."

Key was dumbfounded. Somewhere inside he had always known this could be true. He had always *hoped* it was true. Why had he not realized sooner? Lorn's anger, the whispers, the feeling of always being an outcast. And the thought that his real father could be out there somewhere in the universe was mind-blowing. Could it be true? There were still so many questions, and maybe they would find answers at The Blue Coast, if they made it. Regardless, Key felt no pity for Lorn.

"I don't know what to believe anymore," Key said. "But it's his now, he can have it. He can have everything. The loss, the regret. It's his turn to carry the guilt."

Aurora rested her head on Key's shoulder and nodded. Lorn's fate was not her concern. She didn't expect to feel sadness at their departure, but there it was, tugging at her heart.

"Bye, mama. Bye, daddy," she whispered. Key squeezed her hand.

They watched as the island grew smaller and smaller in the distance. Key had never seen it from such an angle before. It was actually quite beautiful- the wet stones shimmering in shades of orange, the cliffs that hung over the sea. But mostly he was surprised by how small Graystone really was from a distance, how almost non-existent it seemed.

They watched until the island was barely visible, and when nothing was left but a smidgen of orange glow, Key raised his hand in the wind and waved goodbye.

EPILOGUE

Were it not for the colorful houses that dotted the shoreline beside majestic sailboats, The Blue Coast would have simply been *blue*. Fleets of sailboats lined its shores, camouflaging it with the turquoise sea. But those houses- the brightly painted cottages that dotted the cliffs, the pale pink cape homes nestled in the rocks, they upset the blue balance of the coastline, so approaching ships couldn't help but notice it.

There was a commotion on the southern docks today, and Blue Coast villagers were gathered around, eager to catch a glimpse of the excitement. Many of them were delighted, laughing and smiling. Some of them were clutching papers and grinning widely. The Blue Coast was a vast island, but word traveled quickly near the docks, and a crowd was forming around something or someone new. Everyone wanted to know what was going on.

So many villagers had inexplicably gathered by the docks that the Commissioner of Blue Coast Trade had been called. It was his duty to oversee the docks and make sure that trade was fair and orderly. It was also his job to chase off unwanted visitors and vagrants who sought to disrupt the harmony of The Blue Coast (although, truthfully, this didn't happen often).

"You, there!" the Trade Commissioner called to a small, blonde boy walking away from the crowd. "What's all the commotion? What have you got there?"

The boy was smiling ear to ear, staring at the paper in his hand. The Trade Commissioner tugged at the paper and the boy reluctantly let it go.

"Hey!" the boy said. "That's mine, give it back!"

The Trade Commissioner raised his brow and the boy lowered his head. "I'm sorry, Commissioner. May I please have that back?"

The Commissioner stared at the paper. It was a pencil drawing of the little boy, a perfect likeness, down to the cowlick sticking up on the back of his head. The Commissioner was amazed.

"Where did you get this?"

"From the visitor on the docks. He's drawing. He's drawing everything! He's charging ten coins but he gave me mine for free."

The Commissioner looked up and squinted, but he couldn't see anything over the crowd that had gathered on the docks. He handed the drawing back to the boy and ruffled his hair, heading down the dock to the visitor.

"Step aside, please," the Commissioner said, parting the crowd. "Please, folks, Trade Commission coming through."

The Blue Coast villagers respectfully stepped aside, and as the crowd parted, the Commissioner came upon a teenage boy sketching in front of a docked dinghy. A pretty young girl, possibly from The Green Islands, watched affectionately, smiling and collecting payment for the drawings he was providing. The Commissioner opened his mouth to speak, but hesitated when he caught sight of a small notebook, tucked in the boy's bag. He hadn't seen it in many years, but he would recognize that notebook anywhere. The Commissioner's eyes drifted to the old dinghy, and his heart began pounding as he studied it.

He stood behind the sketching artist, unsure if he should speak. It was hard to get the words out, so he cleared his throat.

"Key?" The Commissioner said.

The girl's smile vanished and the boy immediately stopped sketching. The girl touched the boy's shoulder, never taking her eyes off of The Commissioner.

Key already knew, even before he turned his head. He recognized the voice in an instant. He had talked to Aurora about the possibilities before they arrived at The Blue Coast, but he wasn't certain who or what they would find. He put his pencil down and stood to face The Commissioner. He looked him straight in the eye, and now he was certain.

"Hi, London," Key said. He exhaled, feeling the weight of the world slide off of his shoulders. "I missed you."

Acknowledgements

The story of Key and Aurora has been hiding under my bed for decades, and it might still be there if not for the support of many.

My husband, thank you for supporting this dream of mine and for being my best friend, my rock and my partner. You make life better in so many ways and I love you so much.

My son, you are my key to everything. I love you and I'm so grateful to be your mom. Thank you for being the amazing person you are.

My parents and sister, thank you for being such a loving family and supporting me through the years. I am so blessed to have grown up in a home where imagination flourished and books were plentiful (with so many trips to the library!).

Glenn Coats, where would I be without you? I am forever grateful for your encouragement, suggestions, editorial skills, writing magic, and friendship. Thank you for helping to make this dream a reality.

Jenn T, my dear friend and final draft reader, I am so grateful! Thank you for making me believe in myself and for all of your encouragement and enthusiasm. Key and Aurora are here! Finally, the world can meet them.

Danielle, thank you for years of encouragement and fun breakfasts and being the kind and loving friend you are. Let's go buy some aquarium plants to celebrate!

Michele, thank you for being such an amazing friend and my unofficial copy editor. What a gift you are! I am so grateful to have you as a friend. I wish you lived next door.

My teachers here and beyond, thank you: Mrs. Pacca for the story box, Mr. Williams for telling me, "this *will* happen," Mr. Carroll for my first writing award, and Father McCarty, for the 5.0's that made me believe in myself as a writer (even during my unpolished college days).

Sara Francis and Tara September, the tips you gave me were just the push I needed to jump off the high dive. Thank you both for your advice.

Mary and Irene, my Writer's Collective, thank you for your wisdom, suggestions, critiques, and all of the laughs. I am so grateful for you – so many years, so many memories. Cheers to letting our wild inner artists shine! Finally. The journey sure was worth it.

Nicole C, thank you for being one of the first people to believe in my writing and for appreciating stories as gifts. Looks like we both found the way "up there."

And finally, thank you to the many indie writers and creators who were kind enough to share their knowledge and expertise on social media and YouTube. These videos, reels and websites allow writers all over the world to make their own dreams come true in the publishing world. Long live the writers, artists and dreamers!

About the Author

Deborah Zelasny has been writing stories since she was a small child, and most of those stories are still in boxes under her bed. She is a former school teacher and currently owns and operates The Jersey Momma, a travel, lifestyle and entertainment website for fun-seekers of all ages. She resides in the magical land of New Jersey with her husband, son, and emotionally needy dog, Spot. *Key of the Darkhouse* is her first novel. You can keep up with Deborah and all of her antics at JerseyMommaMedia.com or follow her on her social channels, @TheJerseyMomma and on Instagram, @AuthorDeborahZ